Undying Fire

Robin Joy Wirth

Dedication

I am very pleased and excited to say this book is a product of the NaNoWriMo writing event held in November of 2012, of which I am a winner. It would not exist but for that wonderful challenge.

Copyright 2013: Robin Joy Wirth

ISBN-13: 978-1495993534

ISBN-10: 1495993531

Chapter One

Harley Trent's eyes shifted back and forth erratically as his sleeping form squirmed beneath the warmth of his blankets. He was having quite a dream. In his mind's eye he was surrounded by a crush of blackness, like time ebbing away into the stillness of empty space. It was cold, heartless, unfeeling void, and he didn't want to be there.

From the corner of his eye he saw wispy tendrils of vapor begin to form. The chill grew even colder. Then, as he stood there watching, a strange sense of fear began to form. He tried to see in all directions at once, but there was nothing to see. No light, no sound, nothing.

His heart pounded wildly in his chest. Danger circled all around him as thick fog seeped in on his addled consciousness, ebbing and flowing frantically until he realized it had come to surround him in its own right. Somehow its very presence comforted him, as if he was no longer alone in the dark.

He seemed to be in another place and time, possibly in the streets of some older city like Paris or London, but the images were too scattered and fleeting for him to comprehend them. He had no way to determine his exact location. Then, from somewhere behind him, he sensed a familiar presence. He heard a soft, plaintive voice entreating him.

"Don't go," said a beautiful woman with platinum hair and eyes almost the shade of gold. She floated over to him as if she weighed nothing at all, and lovingly wrapped him into her arms.

"What is wrong, Vivianne?" he wanted to know. "I can see by your eyes that you are troubled, my love. But truly, I have everything under control."

"I have a bad feeling about this," she whispered against his lips. "If you face him now, you will not survive the night."

He set her at arm's length and paused to drink in the sight of her. She was the most beautiful woman in existence. Long, flowing hair fell into her eyes and he brushed it aside so he could look into their amber depths.

She looked back at him with tears streaking down her face, which he kissed away with tender care.

"Vivianne, I love you with all my heart, but it is time to put an end to his reign of terror once and for all," he insisted.

"And I love you, husband," she whispered. "I have always loved you. Will you show me your love once more before you die?"

"Do not tempt me, woman," he said. "You know how easily I could be swayed."

"Please, appease my aching heart," she whispered. "For I will have no husband to comfort me after this."

Suddenly the dream shifted. The two of them were naked in the grass that lay beneath the fog. Her amber eyes glinted with mischief as she slowly kissed her way down his body and took his manhood into her mouth, teasing it mercilessly.

"Vixen," he said as he plunged his hands into her white-gold mane of curls. "You are too beautiful for words, my wife."

"Then use your mouth for other things instead," she suggested as she smiled around his hardened flesh and then used her sweet pink tongue to caress it.

"So that's what you want me for, is it?" he teased, drawing her up to kiss her lips. "I'm nothing but your plaything."

"You are so much more than that," she told him then. "You are the only reason my heart continues to beat. If ever I lost you, I could not bear it. Tell me you won't go?"

"I cannot tell you that," he said, though he was very sorry to do so. Her eyes fell from his face, but then the impish twinkle returned as she suddenly mounted him and began to ride. He chuckled, and asked, "So now I am your steed, that you would ride me?"

"I'll ride you and ride you and ride you, until we are far from this place," she answered.

"If you did that, he would surely just find us again."

They made love in earnest then, taking their short time to heights of bliss no man should ever be allowed to endure. But after a time, they knew that they must part. At least until the business was done. After one more lingering kiss he set her away from him, set his shoulders with determination, and disappeared into the mist.

Somewhere in the deep, a voice sounded, cruel and sinister. "I should have taken care of you long ago," he growled with fury. "A mistake I intend to remedy right now."

Harley trembled at the sound of that voice, a voice he had heard often in his dreams, and which he felt an overwhelming desire to quiet forever.

Turning about in slow circles, his eyes took in everything and nothing all at once, the landscape somehow too surreal to be comprehended.

"It won't be as easy as you seem to believe, my Lord," Harley shouted into the nothingness, and pulled free the long wooden stake he had sheathed in a hilt at his side. "I'm not the untried youth you once took under your wing. I am a man. I am more than a man; I am an immortal. You cannot kill what is meant to last forever."

"You cannot escape your destiny," said his enemy, and attacked from out of nowhere. They grappled each other, vying for dominance. As they fought his opponent bared his teeth and they became huge fangs. Startled for a moment, Harley lost his footing, and the next thing he knew his own stake pierced through his heart and exited out his back.

A long, low wail escaped him as he fell to his knees. Pain erupted in his chest, and he felt his life ebbing away as he grasped the bloodied end of the only weapon that could cause him harm.

A piercing scream sounded from somewhere behind him, and his wife ran to his side. He knew in that moment that his enemy had succeeded in his ultimate goal—to separate them. He fell to the unseen earth, writhing in agony.

"No!" shouted his wife as she came to take his head in her delicate hands. "You cannot die, you will not. I will seek and seek until I find the soul that will live again."

"My love for you is undying," he said on a gasp, and felt blood welling up into his throat from the effort, and then felt himself floating away.

"You have not won, my Lord!" Vivianne shouted in the distance. "I will find him again."

"We shall see," the man laughed

wickedly as he grabbed her by the arm. "But for now, you are with me."

Harley awoke with a start, back in the world of the living. The alarm clock was blaring loudly, and he fumbled to turn it off.

With a shuddering sigh, Harley reflected on the number of nights he had seen that tear-streaked face in his dreams. It seemed as if the woman had haunted him all his life, almost every night that he could remember. She was as familiar to him as any person he saw in his waking life, and far more dear to him than anyone else he could think of.

"Too bad she isn't real," he told himself in the mirror as he started to shave away the dark brown stubble that had grown overnight. He nicked himself and swore softly. As he fumbled for a small sliver of toilet paper he reflected back on his life.

He had been in a relationship or two during his thirty-five years, and he had even tried his hand at marriage for a while, but it always seemed like nobody could supplant the dream in his heart. He always felt as though she was the part of him that was missing, and he longed to find her so he could finally be whole.

Melancholy thoughts aren't going to help you," he muttered into the mirror. "She's a dream, and you need to forget her." And with an effort, he changed his thoughts to a more useful topic.

Harley had just made Lead Detective, and today was to be his first day on the new job. He was excited, for he had worked hard to achieve the position. He could hardly wait to take charge of the team he had been a member of for the past ten years. And he knew that most of them were unlikely to give him a bad time.

He donned his best suit for a moment, but decided he looked too stupid in it. He was going to work, not a wedding. Taking off the white shirt and tie and foregoing the jacket in favor of a comfortable black shirt, he nodded with satisfaction as he headed for the door, jangling his car keys all the way out to his car.

Chapter Two

With perhaps a slightly over-inflated sense of pride, Lead Detective Harley Trent walked briskly through the station and into his newly painted office for the first time. He glanced with a bit of pride at the name on the door—Detective Harley Trent. He held his smile in check as he looked inside.

His eye fell upon each item within with a small joy leaping about in his heart. He was well pleased with the large desk and the comfortable chair he found inside, and he could hardly wait to get started.

This office was a man's office, painted in warm brown tones, with stark white blinds on the windows, and shelves made of a dark cherry wood. On the desk was perched a state of the art computer which prominently took up most of the space on one side. There were so many drawers for odds and ends he thought he'd died and gone to heaven.

He could definitely learn to like the place.

Del Brucco, a junior detective and longtime friend, sauntered in right behind him, oohing and aahing the whole way. He took in Harley's smile with a happy contentment born of the fact that his friend saw him smile so much quite rarely.

"Now isn't this nice? Mm-hm. Are you enjoying your first day on the new job, Mr. Lead Detective Harley Trent?" he said conversationally. "How does it feel to finally be number one?"

"Feels good," Harley said in smooth tones as he took a seat in his patent leather office chair. He moved around a bit, adjusting until he found just the right spot as he leaned back. When he was completely comfortable and had the computer's monitor exactly where he wanted it, he added, "Real good."

"Well, I'm glad you think so, detective," said Mary Wright as she walked in with a rather large file in one hand and an even bigger cup of coffee in the other. "I thought you might need this. It's every file we have on the current case."

"Sounds like I might need the coffee, too."

Harley cast his friend a knowing glance, and the black man grinned momentarily as he checked out Mary's tight buns while her back was to him. She set down the file and the coffee, bending over more than strictly necessary as she winked at Harley.

Pretending not to notice, Harley had to stifle a chuckle at Del's expense. Mary was a thin, willowy woman with flowing red hair and green eyes, and even Trent had to admit she was fine to look at. Not really a woman to his tastes, since he inherently seemed to prefer blondes, but still fine in her own right.

"That could be construed as sexual harassment, Detective Brucco," she said sweetly as she patted Del on the cheek and swiftly walked out and in again with a cup for him. "You may as well stay here. We've got another body."

"A man can't help ogling at least a little when confronted with something that looks that good," Del excused himself amiably as he pulled up a chair and sat in it backwards. "And you even remembered just how I like my coffee. I love a woman who remembers the little things—it shows how much she cares."

"Not one bit, you horny rascal," Mary laughed, and turned back to the folder on the desk, opening it to the most recent entry. "Gentlemen, it seems our killer struck again just two nights ago. Here is all the data we have collected so far. You may want to familiarize yourselves with the rest of the information as well, even though I know you've been following this case for some time now."

"Yes, we worked on the last killing under Jefferson, so it's all still fresh in our minds," Del said.

"You never can tell if you overlooked some small detail that will bust this thing wide open," Mary reminded him.

"I won't need to go over most of it," Harley said. "I know everything there is to know about all the cases but the newest one."

"I thought you might say that. Here are the new photos. Notice the strange wounds on the neck, very similar to those found on the other six. For lack of any better explanation, forensics has determined that they are bite marks of some kind, but they don't believe an animal was involved."

"Reminds me of that vampire flick I was watching the other night," Del mentioned with a click of his tongue. "But we all know there's no such thing as vampires in real life. I mean, how could they exist in this day and age without us knowing, right?

At this, Harley's gaze became speculative as he stared at the recent photo. Despite everything he'd ever been told about vampires being a myth, the look of the mark on this woman's neck did indeed look suspiciously like the bites shown in classic vampire movies—except that they had been inflicted with a much more brutal force.

Whoever had done this, they seemed to be taking a great deal of pleasure in it. Only someone completely inhuman would tear open another person's throat like that.

"I don't know," he said as he leaned forward in this chair with tented hands. "There are some pretty weird people on the streets of Los Angeles. Even if we rule out the possibility of real vampires going around the city and sucking people dry, that doesn't rule out the idea entirely."

"Oh, here we go," said Del as he rolled his eyes. "Leave it to Trent to take a joke and turn it into something serious."

"Maybe this guy believes himself to be a vampire, whether he actually is one or not," Harley pointed out. "I've heard of those types hanging around near the Hollywood sign in some club they frequent. It might be worth looking into."

"Look at the big bad detective," said Del with a laugh. "You must not want to keep your job very long, coming up with cork-brained theories like that one. So you think some wannabe vampire is going around brutalizing the populace? Almost sounds like you want vampires to be real to me."

"Come on, Del, think about it. It makes sense," Harley defended himself. "Look at all the evidence. Every one of the bodies slain in the same way, their throats literally torn open. Mary, set all those photos up on the board, please. I'd like to have a look at them in order of occurrence."

Del put up his hands. "Don't do it on my account. I'm not the one you're going to have to sell this shit to."

"I wouldn't even try," Harley assured him. "But you know that I've mentioned this idea before to Jefferson, and he thought it was implausible as well. The fact of the matter is, nothing else we've been trying has panned out. We need a new angle."

"Making the implausible plausible," Del chuckled. "That's one way to do it."

"Where's that map showing where all the attacks occurred?" Harley asked Mary, and she quickly found it and put it up on the board as well. "Look here, Del, doesn't it seem like a highly localized area? I wonder if there's some kind of weird cult down there."

"Trent, be reasonable," he protested. "There are weird cults all over the city. I happen to know there's a really big gang of thieves that call themselves the Trid not five miles from here."

"But they're not likely to go out and tear someone's throat open and drink out all their blood," he pointed out. "The worst they get up to is throwing raves and kidnapping hookers to service them there. I'm not interested in them. I'm looking for something much more specific. Any cults whose followers actually believe they are vampires or werewolves, or that sort of thing. Any cults that like feasting on human blood."

"Sounds like you've got your first day of work cut out for you," Del told him. "Anything I can do to help?"

"I want to go see the most recent crime scene," he answered. "Let's see if we can turn up any clues."

"You're the boss—*boss*," he said with a salute. "Let's get truckin'."

Chapter Three

"We need the top floor, please," Harley told the elevator operator as they stepped into the velvet-lined, plush-carpeted enclosure. The man nodded and pushed the button in question. He eyed the two men speculatively, obviously having figured out who they were.

"So, you guys are going to try to figure out what happened to Sally Ross?" he asked finally.

"Yes, sir," Harley answered. "Did you know the victim?"

"Oh, yes. Been shuttling her up to the top for years now" he assured him. "She's been hanging around with some really weird types lately. God only knows if any one of them might have done her in." "Weird types?" Harley questioned. "What do you mean, weird types?"

"A whole lot of men, all dressed in black; pale skinned, and they never came to see her except at night," he explained. "That's what really got me thinking, those men were all kind of creepy. Vampire types. There's no other way to describe them, really."

Harley and Del exchanged a look.

"Did one of these weird vampire types come to see her the night she died?" Harley wanted to know.

"Three of them did, each at a different time. Honestly I was starting to wonder if she was exchanging sex for something else—but I'm not sure what it would be. Sally wasn't into drugs, and she didn't tend to gamble either." he said. "Besides which, after she started having them over, she got more and more pale herself, like maybe there was something wrong with her. And no wonder—I think she may have been giving them her blood."

"You're that certain these men seemed like vampires?" Harley asked. "Did any one of them seem more violent looking that the others?"

"No, sorry, they were all too creepy in my book," he said with a shudder. "I had a fear for my own neck whenever they were around."

"Well, thank you," Harley said, handing him a card. "I'd like you to go down to the station and give a statement, if you will. Your information could prove very helpful in the case."

"I'll do that just as soon as I finish my shift," the man agreed as he put the card into a pocket in his shirt. "Top floor."

The doors opened and the two men stepped out into the long, gilded hall. It was easy to determine which suite to approach. The door was crisscrossed with bright yellow tape with the words 'crime scene' written all over it. The two nodded to each other and made their way to the door.

As they approached the entrance the door suddenly creaked open all by itself, making each man jump backwards and unholster his gun, aiming at the movement. Then they realized no one was there and put their weapons away again.

The sight that met them was both shocking and no real surprise at the same time. The walls were covered with pictures of the undead, and the room was accented with statuary of the same nature. Over the mantle hung a large painting of a horde of hell beasts feeding in a very graphic display.

As he looked closely at the paintings, Harley noticed something odd. One of them, the one just to the right of the centerpiece, was of the Madonna and Child.

"How odd," he said, pointing it out.

"What's odd?" asked Del.

"Why would an obviously vampirically obsessed, undead loving sort of a girl need to display a clearly Catholic picture on her wall?"

"Maybe she was raised Catholic?" Del suggested.

"Hmm," Harley said noncommittally. He scanned each of the rooms meticulously, looking for clues. No blood, not even that of the deceased, marred any floor. The woman had been found lying in her bed, and that area was also devoid of blood. However, he did find a sliver of black material hidden under her pillow.

"Hand me a specimen bag," he instructed Del, and his friend complied. He pulled some tweezers out of his pocket and used them to put the black material in the bag. Then he deftly sealed it and handed it back to Del.

"Okay, get the camera ready, Del," he said. "I want to see if anything is under the bed."

Del filmed as Harley examined the floor under the bed. As an afterthought, he flipped the mattress on end and looked there as well. Eyes wide with horrified surprise, he said, "Del, get a close-up."

As Del filmed, Harley meticulously picked up eight bags of blood, one at a time, and put them all into a large bag to bring back to the lab.

"Why would this be under here?" Del asked as he shook his head. "You don't think it's her blood, do you?"

"We won't know until it gets analyzed," Harley told him. "But at a guess, I doubt it. Why would someone go to the trouble of draining her and then leave the blood behind?"

"But why would someone want to hide somebody else's blood under their victim's mattress either?" Del pointed out.

"The man we're dealing with is obviously a psychopath," Harley pointed out. "Maybe he just wanted to get the evidence out of his possession before someone discovered it. It could very well belong to one of the other victims. And since we have eight victims and eight bags of blood, I'd lay bets on those things each belonging to one of them."

"Yeah, that's insane all right," Del agreed with a nod.

"Let's get this stuff back to headquarters and call it a day," Harley said.

"You know, that party they're throwing for you tonight should be a blast," Del mentioned. "It's not every day a man makes Lead Detective. I hope you're going to be more sociable than you normally are."

Harley snorted ruefully. "Since when am I not sociable?"

"You, my friend, are a total stick in the mud," Del told him. "Every time you come to a social gathering I know right where to find you—in some dark corner brooding about something or other. At least have a drink or two, dance with some of the ladies. It won't kill you to have a good time."

Harley's brow was furrowed as his eyes took in everything around him. "Whoever killed this woman, she must have let them in," he said. "The only sign of a possible struggle is in that bag. How can you expect me to have fun until I know what we're dealing with?"

"We'll have to wait for forensics to have a look just like you said," Del reminded him. "About the fabric, though, do you think it could have come from a black coat—like the ones the so-called vampire cult wears?"

"Could be," Harley agreed. "Well, I've seen enough here, we can head back home to get ready once the evidence is in good hands."

"All right," Del agreed. "Why don't you head on home right now? I can turn the evidence in by myself."

"I think I will," Harley agreed as they went their separate ways.

Chapter Four

The sun was just setting as Harley Trent, dressed all in his usual dark tones, stepped back out of the lobby to his fifth floor condominium and ambled out onto the trash-littered sidewalk. He headed for his car, which was parked a few yards away in a numbered parking lot.

He was speculating on the dream he'd had during his light doze. The dreams of Vivianne were becoming more intense than ever, and he caught himself holding his breath as he thought of her delectable curves. Why, oh why couldn't she be real?

Then Harley's nostrils flared, as if he sensed something odd in the air and couldn't quite place it. An eerie chill made him shiver, and instinctively he glanced down at his feet, looking for fog.

This is reality, he reminded himself. The fog won't show up in real life, any more than the woman. Still, there was a brief moment when he could not help but turn and look in every direction, just in case.

When he spotted someone further up the road he knew his senses had been correct. The same feeling he got in his dreams accosted his senses— the same sense he always felt whenever his enemy was present. On the sidewalk, about ten yards away, a strange looking man approached.

What made him stand out, exactly? He wore a long, black trench coat and a pair of sunglasses. His dark hair was spiked, and he had one ear pierced. It sported a dangling earring of some kind, but Harley wasn't close enough to see what the emblem was.

So why had he triggered his senses? He'd seen plenty of men dressed like this one, but there was a sense of danger surrounding him. Somehow the set of his shoulders and the look on his face combined to create a formidable force.

Unaccountably, Harley felt the need to hurry to his car to avoid the man, almost fearful in his attempt. He sat in the driver's seat and started the ignition, and just then the man passed by. He flipped down his sunglasses to look in at Harley. His eyes were black as sin, but the pupils shone a bright red.

Every muscle in Harley's body froze until the man had passed completely. When he was gone, Harley finally backed out his black sedan and headed over to the bar where his party was to be held.

Del was right about one thing, he decided. Being the Lead Detective sure was making a big difference in his life. But he wasn't so sure he liked where it was headed if it meant coming across creepy characters like that one.

As he exited his vehicle and headed for the door to the bar, he caught a brief glimpse of a man in a trench coat walking casually towards an alley nearby. A man with dark, spiky hair and sunglasses. But he knew this couldn't possibly be the same man as before—he couldn't walk twenty blocks in ten minutes—no one could.

"Harley?" said Del as he stepped inside. "What's the matter with you? You look as though you've seen a ghost."

"Something like that," he said as he stepped up to the bar. "Hey, barkeep? I could really use a Bloody Mary."

"Certainly, sir," he said. "And since this party is for you, all your drinks tonight are on the house."

"Okay, then I guess you'd better make that two," he said. "For a start."

"Harley, what the hell is going on?" Del insisted as he followed him, drinks in hand, over to one of the booths near the back of the place. "You're not seriously going to just sit back here in the shadows like you always do, are you? This is your party. The least you can do is join us long enough to get congratulated. What's gotten into you?"

"I don't know, Del," he answered as he downed the first drink in one gulp. "Some really freaky stuff has been happening. I can't explain it—it's almost like a physical force. Immense power. I can't shake him, and I don't know what he wants."

"Have you been drinking already, man?"

"No, no," Harley said, holding up his hands to ward off the words. "That's not it."

"Trent, you're not making any sense," he told him. "Maybe you should not tell the others what you just told me. They might decide to take your badge back."

"Very funny, Brucco," Harley growled. "Just remember I'm now in a position to take yours."

"They got you a cake, Harley," Del confided. "The least you can do is come on over and act surprised. Think of it as boosting morale."

"The fact they're at a party at all is sure to boost that," he pointed out.

"Come on, Lead Detective, let's go get it over with."

With a longsuffering sigh, Harley got up and pasted a smile on his face as he went to join the others. They all started singing, "For He's a Jolly Good Fellow," and only one of them was singing it correctly. The cacophony of the chorus rang in his ears, making the fake smile slip away completely by the time the song was done.

"Thank you, people," he said with a staged bow.

Someone put a glass of champagne into his outstretched hand, and then another person shouted, "To Detective Trent, may he lead us to victory over the city of L.A!"

"Oh, now, I wouldn't go that far," Harley said with a blush. "I'm only one man, and this is a really huge city. If it wasn't for all of you underlings working the streets every day, I'd never be up to the task."

"Hear, hear!" Del shouted, raising his glass again.

"Detective, I'm going to let you ask me to dance," Mary told him as she took his glass from his hand, then took the Bloody Mary he was still holding out of the other one. "Come on, just one dance to loosen you up, and then you can turn all that charisma loose on the ladies."

"Ha, ha," he said as they reached the dance floor. "Which one of them do you really think would want to have anything to do with me?"

"What about officer LaSalle?"

"Not my type," he commented, gyrating to the song in the background.

"Oh, why not? She's not emo enough for you?"

"What's that supposed to mean?" he grumbled.

Mary chuckled. "That answer says it all, does it not?"

Rolling his eyes in response, Harley simply said, "I need a drink."

"Thanks for the dance, sir," said Mary as he walked away. "Charming as ever. You've got my vote for hottest guy in the room."

"I'll keep that in mind," he called back as he continued to walk away. Reaching the others, Harley grabbed up his Bloody Mary and the remaining bottle of champagne and headed back over to his corner. For one brief moment, he thought he saw a man in a trench coat and sunglasses seated there, but when he shook his head to clear it, he was gone.

Chapter Five

Harley was totally drunk when he made it home several hours later. After the song subsided and everyone ate cake he had returned to his hiding place and proceeded to anesthetize himself into a state where he could avoid the thoughts plaguing him. Unfortunately, the anesthesia had done its job a bit too well.

Staggering his way to the closet, he hung his jacket up as neatly as he was able, and then headed straight for the porcelain god to pay homage to it. Bloody Mary and champagne, mixed with liberal doses of the drinks his co-workers had bought for him throughout the night, did not have a pleasant taste the second time around.

The room was spinning as he wandered into his bedroom and fell onto the bed, face buried in his pillow and rump up in the air. With a long, low groan, he wondered how soon it would be before he passed out so he didn't have to endure his misery.

He didn't have to wait long, thankfully. Soon his brain spun off into oblivion, and the fog began to roll in just like it always did. Every sound inside his head echoed strangely, disorienting him. Spinning around, he saw nothing that would give him a clue as to the identity of his tormentor.

"What do you want from me?" he shouted within his head. "You already killed me once, why won't you just leave me alone?"

"I want your soul, Detective Trent," echoed a male voice. It was coming from all directions at once, making Harley's dream-self spin in circles yet again, but with no better results than before.

"Tell me, why does this feel so real when it's just a dream? Why do I always dream of you?" he wanted to know. "Please, you've plagued me for so long. Why must you torment me this way?"

"You are not what you should be, Harley. Nothing more, and nothing less. I expected better of you than this farce of an existence."

"And what should I be?" Harley persisted.

"You should be immortal."

"I am immortal," he answered with extreme confidence. "I will always be—"

"You're a fool, Detective Trent," the voice said. "When exactly was it that you became such a fool?"

"Tell me what you mean!"

"Soon your eyes will see that which they could not see," he hissed, the words bouncing all around Harley, not quite understood. "Soon you will become what you once had been. That is your fate, Detective. I have been looking for you since the day you were born. Our minds are still bound because of the past. This body is stronger than the last. Perhaps this time you will be strong enough to survive."

"Get out of my head, you bastard!"

"Soon," the voice echoed once more, and then faded away into the shadows of his mind.

)0(

Harley looked at himself in the mirror as he trudged into the bathroom the next morning. This case was really getting to him, giving him nightmares.

And now he was more involved with it than ever. Fully shaved and often nicked, he trudged into the living room, tiny bits of white tissue dotting his chin and neck, and decided to check his latest messages.

Most of them were unremarkable, until the last one played. It was Mary.

"Detective Trent, our stalker has been at it again," she informed him. "This one's a bit different. You may want to come in as soon as possible to see this."

"Damn!"

Harley dressed as fast as he could, made himself a quick cup of coffee from the still-hot liquid from the day before, and then ran around looking for his keys for ten minutes before he was able to find them in his coat pocket. Throwing on the comfortable brown coat, he went out onto the sidewalk, not bothering to look for his stalker this time in his haste.

Harley crashed right into the trench coat guy, then backed away to apologize. "Sorry, sir. I didn't realize you were there."

"Sometimes your eyes cannot see what is right before you," he replied in a strangely foreign accent. "Personally, I cannot abide to look at the sun, and I only tolerate it when I must. Good day, Detective Trent. And good luck with your newly appointed position."

"Yes, good day," he answered as he headed toward his car. Then he stopped short and turned around again. The man was nowhere to be seen. "Wait, how do you know I'm a detective?" he called out, but of course there was no answer. Shaken, Harley sat in the driver's seat and took a few deep breaths before he turned the key.

"Maybe I'm just going crazy," he muttered as the engine revved.

"Maybe you are," the man answered as he stood beside the driver's side door smirking. He held a cigarette between his lips and lit it with a match. "There is always that possibility."

Before Harley could even respond, the man disappeared again. Harley floored it as he backed out, and then he drove to the station at a much quicker pace than necessary.

Once he was there, Harley breezed past all the greetings and headed directly into his office. Within moments, Mary was there with coffee and updates, and he settled back into his daily routine of tracking a killer. Del and two other members of his team, Scott and Allen Piper, came along with him. They all stood gaping at the pictures Mary was arranging on the wall. Gruesome did not begin to describe the carnage.

"My God," Scott gasped as he stared. "No man could be capable of doing something like that. How could anyone allow themselves to sink so low?"

"Okay, calm down, people," Harley said. "Let's try to get past the emotional response and get down to the cold, hard facts."

"Yes, sir," the others chimed.

"Mary, another coffee would be good," he mentioned as he smiled at the woman. She got up to get it for him, bringing in the entire pot and shutting the door behind her. Then she pulled the shades while she was at is as she noticed some of the officers glancing in.

"Do you have the pathology report for this victim yet?" he inquired.

"The body is in the forensics lab right now," Mary answered. "But first, you need to know where this one was found. Sir, I don't know where she was killed, but she was found in your next door neighbor's condo."

"Impossible," he said. "I would have heard something."

"Yes, unless you were passed out drunk," she answered as she took in the dark circles under his eyes.

"Well," he said. "There is always that possibility."

Chapter Six

With some curiosity, Harley walked into the morgue section in the basement of the Forensics building that neighbored the police station. His nerves were still a bit of jangled from his most recent dream, as it had seemed more real than those he'd had before.

Worse than that, Vivianne had not come to offer comfort this time. He wondered what had happened to her, where she might have been instead.

But then he reminded himself that she hadn't gone anywhere at all, because she was just a figment of his overactive imagination. He really needed to just let the whole thing go. What was the point in dwelling on dreams?

He knew from the photographs he'd viewed this morning that the body he was about to go see was quite mangled. This was the part of his new position he had not been looking forward to—actually being the one to go down for a look.

Thankfully, that had been Jefferson's task until now. They had never really discussed the topic, even though they talked frequently about a lot of things. It felt very odd being in the station without him. Harley hadn't realized he'd miss the old man so much.

Inside the office, a young receptionist sat painting her nails and chewing gum. She snapped it loudly as she looked up and noticed that she was no longer alone. "Can I help you?" she asked as she removed her gum with a thumb and forefinger and straightened into a more professional pose.

"Yes, you can," he said. "I haven't been down here before. Could you direct me to the autopsy section?"

"Right through that door, sir," she said with a big smile. "I guess you must be the new top dog."

"Yes," he agreed absent-mindedly as a wave of nausea hit him. The smell coming from the room she'd indicated could gag a maggot.

"Oh yeah, I almost forgot," she said as she noticed his discomfort. "Better put some of this in your nostrils before you go."

Harley took the little bottle and dabbed some of its contents under his nose. "Thanks," he said as he returned it to her.

"No problem," she said conversationally. "That's my personal stash, you know. It's not an easy job sitting just outside a room full of stiffs every day."

"Yes, I can imagine," he said, and then headed for the door she'd indicated.

"Good luck in there," the girl called after him, and he waved back at her before he turned the knob.

Just as he'd expected, the place was fairly immaculate, with white walls and a white-tiled floor. All the sheets in sight appeared to be white as well. Harley wondered if there was some significance to the fact.

A body lay front and center on one of the tables. It was completely covered by one of the white sheets, and he didn't see anyone else in the room. Surreptitiously, he moved to the gurney and lifted one edge of the fabric to see who was under there. It was a man's body—clearly not the one he'd come to see.

"May I help you?" said a decidedly feminine voice from

somewhere behind him. Jumping like a kid caught with his hand in the cookie jar, Harley turned about to face the woman he hadn't noticed before.

"Yes," he answered sheepishly. "I'm Detective Trent. I've come to have a look at the remains of Amanda Beckett. It's part of the Slayer case."

"Oh, yes," she said in an accent he couldn't quite place. "I'm Anne Salvo, Detective. They told me you would be coming. Miss Beckett is to be next on the block after this guy. Would you like to wait out in the hall until it's time?"

"If you don't mind, I'd kind of like to stay," he said. "I've never seen an autopsy in person before." Harley was staring at the woman. There was something familiar about her. It was as though he knew her face, and knew her voice. He had visions within his mind of her sitting on top of him, undulating in the throes of an intense passion. Shaking his head vigorously to rid it of such lascivious thoughts, Harley tried to focus all his attention on her words instead of her delectable anatomy.

"So, Detective Trent," she said as she walked over to uncover the dead man's head. "How long have you had this morbid fascination with cadavers?"

"You're teasing me," he said with a smirk.

"Not really," she said, smiling now. "You see, I myself have been fixated on death for a very long time. I find it fascinating how one moment you're inside of a body, and the next you just—aren't. Don't you ever wonder where your essence goes once it has left its body?"

"I—I don't suppose I've given much thought to the matter," he responded. "My parents are devout Catholics, you see, but I was never able to share their enthusiasm for the church. We haven't spoken in many years."

"Perhaps that is all to the good," she answered in a rather cryptic manner.

"How do you mean?" Harley asked.

"Parents can be such a bother when you don't follow in their footsteps," she said. "If you're going to stand there, you may as well make yourself useful. Hand me that scalpel, please."

Harley looked down at the tray and her gloved hands, and asked, "Should I put on gloves first?"

"Yes, that's always a good idea," she answered as she pulled out a small recorder and pressed a button.

"John Doe 15248, cause of death probably homicide. The body appears to be predominantly in good shape except for several broken bones and severe lacerations conducive to being thrown out of a tenth story window, as witnesses have described." Harley located the boxes of gloves and grabbed a pair from the one marked 'large'. He slid them on as she continued speaking in the recorder, and picked up the scalpel she'd asked for.

Anne took the scalpel from him as she turned on a video camera just behind him. "Detective Harley Trent is assisting me at this time. I'm now going to open the chest cavity to have a look." She made a long incision and then turned to grab some strange looking contraption she used to open the chest cavity in the blink of an eye.

"You're pretty good at that," Harley commented.

"Comes with practice," she answered through the facemask she'd pulled down over her nose and mouth. "I'm good at a lot of things, Detective."

"I'll bet you are," he answered appreciatively. Their eyes met over top of the body and then simultaneously they both remembered that they were in a less than romantic setting at the moment, and Anne blushed as she turned back to her work.

"Nothing unexpected in there," she commented dryly. "There's no point in opening the head, looks like the fall did it already."

"Yes, so it would seem."

They went on in this manner for about an hour before she declared the autopsy to be concluded. Then she called in some assistants to remove John Doe and replace him with the body of Amanda Beckett.

"Well," she said. "That was a good training session. Now for the real thing."

Chapter Seven

Anne and Harley stood off to the side and waited as a couple of techs came in and removed John Doe and brought out the next body. Though they did not speak, the silence was a companionable one rather than uncomfortable, as was often the case when two people first met.

The two suited up with new gloves, and Anne even got Harley a smock to put over his clothes. Amanda Beckett's body had so many injuries to document that the two spent almost two hours of intensive work to catalogue them all.

Harley couldn't help but ask, "So, Anne, just exactly how did you get into this line of work? I mean, it's not a job most women dream of, is it?"

Anne chuckled. "Well, no, I suppose not."

"So, why did you?"

"It's sort of a family tradition," she said as she stepped back and pulled off her gloves, which were too bloody to work with, and pulled on another pair. Harley got another pair for himself as well.

"As I said, death and I have had a strange sort of relationship for a very long time. Before I finished schooling, I used to be a forensic make-up artist, but I got tired of trying to make them look pretty and decided to learn how to determine what messed them up to begin with. It seemed logical if you think about it. After all, without purpose, a being ceases to be useful. Generally speaking, I prefer to have a purpose, myself."

"That makes sense, somehow," Harley said. "Miss Salvo, can we have a closer look at those bite marks on her throat? I'd like to determine if they were made by an animal or a human."

"Of course, detective," she agreed as she reached for a long, slender instrument from the tray. "Do you see this? It's a tool to measure the depth of the wound. This is a piercing wound that went in approximately one and a half inches, but then it looks as though the attacker must have been interrupted soon after the penetration. It's the only explanation I can think of for the apparent violence of the tearing action when compared to the other victims."

"You don't believe the killer is just becoming more violent, Miss Salvo?" he asked her then. " I think the wounds have been becoming progressively worse over time."

"That's one theory, I suppose, but it seems inconsistent with his activity prior to the last two bodies," she said. "But what really concerned me the most about this body in particular were all the other bites and scratches. They all appear to have occurred while she was still alive, but I don't see how one killer could have inflicted all of them in so short a time span."

"So you're saying you believe the killer might be more than one individual?" Harley asked. "That's a theory I haven't heard before. How long have you been on this case, anyway, if you don't mind my asking?"

"A couple of months now," she told him. "Long enough to be the one who got to test out those bags of blood you found, and determining they all came from the same victim. And that the victim they came from was not the one found at that crime scene."

"That's unexpected," Harley commented speculatively.

"Yes. However, I haven't gotten back the data from all the samples I took when Miss Beckett here arrived. The data sequencer won't be complete for several more hours. I think we can close up this little session for now."

"All right," Harley agreed as he stripped off his gloves. "I could use a good, stiff drink. How about you, Miss Salvo?"

"Are you asking me out, Detective Trent?" Anne smirked as she removed her gloves.

"Yes, I am, Miss Salvo."

"Then don't you think you ought to start calling me Anne?"

"Okay, Anne," he said with a blush.

"Well, since you've already been initiated into my world a little, there'd be no harm in drawing you in a little further, right?" she asked as she pulled off her hat and mask. A gorgeous mane of platinum blonde curls sprang free and fell down the length of her back.

"What did you have in mind?" he asked as his heart skipped a beat.

"Let's go get that drink in The Bloody Harlot tavern."

"You've got to be kidding," Harley scoffed. "What kind of a name is that?"

"Detective, let me ask you something," she said as she strode toward the door, pausing for a moment to call in the techs for clean-up.

"What is it, Anne?" he asked as he followed her.

"I wondered what exactly you think this case is really about," she said. "Have you put together any kind of a theory about the killer?"

"I have come up with one theory," he admitted. "But it seems far-fetched at best."

"And what might that theory be?" Anne removed her gown and tossed it into the laundry, then tossed in her facemask and hat in as well.

"I'm not sure I want to tell you," he admitted. "I'm afraid you'd think I'd lost my mind."

"Try me," she said with a grin.

Harley thought; damn, I'd love to try you. He said, "All right, then. I believe that this killer must be very heavily into the occult. He may be extremely fascinated by the idea of creatures of the night, such as werewolves or vampires. So fascinated, in fact, that he has been acting out those fantasies on the seven women and four men he appears to have slaughtered so far."

"And in the course of all your work, Detective Trent, I'm certain you know that most serial killers tend to stick to a particular type of person—one gender, or a similar look, or maybe a similar profession, is that not right?"

"Yes," he agreed.

"So, since this killer is not particular about who he kills, does it not follow he may just be in it for the hunt?"

"I had said as much to Detective Jefferson myself," Harley agreed.

"And what exactly makes you so sure the killer is pretending to be a supernatural being? What if he really is a werewolf, or more likely, considering the manner of the killings, a vampire?" she asked with a slight smirk.

"And here I thought you were going to be the one thinking I was crazy for suggesting it," Harley scoffed. "But it's not a theory that has been well received by the rest of the team."

"What would you say, Detective Trent, if I told you that your theory is quite credible, because creatures of the night are real?"

"I'd say you've been watching too many old movies, Miss Salvo," he commented with a smirk as they reached the parking lot. "Your car or mine?"

"Actually, I don't have a car, Detective," she informed him. "Usually I get wherever I need to be by bus or on foot."

"Well then, hop in, sweet lady," he said. "I know how to get there—not that I've ever tried before."

Anne laughed at this as she buckled her seat-belt. "Well then, get ready for a real culture shock, Harley Trent. This place is definitely not your average, run-of-the-mill kind of bar."

"I don't know, Miss Salvo," he said. "I've seen some pretty strange places in my time."

With a chuckle, she sat back looked him over for a moment. "Do you know, you're very easy to talk to. That's a nice change."

"Thanks, I think," he answered as he backed the car out and headed for the freeway. Anne sat back and enjoyed the scenery for the twenty minute drive, and from the corner of his eye, so did Harley.

Sleek, that's what he'd call her. From her savvy attitude and her perfect skin, to the sound of her voice as well. She was more beautiful than any woman had a right to be. And he wanted her for himself.

As they got out of the car and stepped into the Bloody Harlot, all such thoughts were wiped away for the moment as he took in his surroundings.

Well, he thought as he took in the black and red draperies and the black-clad patrons inside, I guess I don't have to look too hard to find a hang-out for vampires, because if ever there was such a place, this would be it.

Chapter Eight

Retired Lead Detective Frank Jefferson answered his phone after the third ring. He'd thought that he would never have to hear it ring at all hours of the night once he'd passed on his job to Trent, but so far he had been proven wrong.

However, it was not Trent who kept calling him, it was Mary.

"Hello?" he asked tiredly as he sat back down in his easy chair and used the remote to turn down the volume on the TV. "Retired detective Jefferson here."

Silence.

"Dammit, why call someone if you don't intend to talk to them?" he barked into the receiver, then slammed it down as hard as he could. "Stupid prank callers!"

The phone rang again, and he didn't answer. The next time it rang he picked it up and shouted angrily, "What?"

Again, silence. Then, it rang another three times before he answered again. "You damn well better talk to me this time, you miserable puke, or I'll shove my hand right through the goddam receiver and yank your throat out!"

"Are you alone, Detective?" asked a man in a smooth tone that sent chills down Frank's spine.

"Who the hell is this?" Frank demanded hotly.

"Aw, Detective, you wound me," he answered in an even smoother tone. "I was certain that you would remember the man who has been keeping you and your team so busy for the last five years. How soon they forget. Ah, well, no matter. Time to move on to more important business."

"Slayer?" Frank whispered. Perspiration broke out on his forehead.

"Bingo, Detective Jefferson," said the voice, much more sinister now.

"What do you want with me?" Frank demanded. "I'm no longer on the case. Why aren't you picking on somebody who still gives a damn?"

"Yes, I had heard of your retirement," he cooed. "And thank you, by the way, for training your replacement so very well. Detective Harley Trent is a credit to the force, just like you were. Good job, Frank."

"All right, I've had about enough of this. Just tell me what the hell you want and get it over with," Frank complained. "I'm trying to watch Jeopardy."

"Ah, yes, Jeopardy," he chuckled. "That's what we should do—play a round, just you and I. The answer is, 'dead'?"

"What? What do you mean, dead?" Frank grumbled, and slammed the phone down again. This time he answered right away but said nothing.

"What is the question, Detective?" he insisted. "I've given you the answer, now it's your turn. Can you tell me the question?"

"Why should I? I have no interest in your stupid games."

"Detective, you should play this game with me," he responded. "It may be a matter of life or death. The answer is 'dead'. Tell me the question."

"What are all of your victims?" he asked uncertainly.

"Not precisely, although that's a very good try," he chuckled. "But I'm inclined to be generous tonight. A second chance, perhaps?"

"What is your next victim?" Frank asked, even more uncertain.

"You're getting warmer, Frank," he said in an enigmatic tone. "One more try? Third time's a charm, so they say. What is the question?"

"What is—" Frank began, and then he spotted the dark shadow of a man standing outside the living room window.

A flash of lightning startled him. He hadn't thought that it was raining outside, but he was probably just preoccupied by the phone calls. In the distance, A dog let out a plaintive howl.

"What is—" he began again, but then stopped abruptly, his jaw dropping to his knees.

The figure now stood inside the window, right behind the drapes.

"What the devil?" Frank growled as he went to grab for his gun.

"Not quite, Frank," growled the figure behind the curtains. "Try again."

"Get out of my house!"

Laughter.

"Don't forget to release the safety, Frank," chuckled the man as the lamp that was lighting the room suddenly sputtered and went out. The shadowy figure crossed the room with catlike grace and stood grinning before him. "Well, Frank, aren't you going to shoot me? I'm standing right here, waiting for it. Go ahead and shoot."

Frank fired off two rounds right into the man's torso. He barely even flinched.

"What's the question, Frank?"

He swallowed hard as he stared up at the creature who stood before him, fangs bared. With a sickened look on his face, he looked down at the useless gun in his hand, and said, "What is 'me'?"

"Bingo!" growled the vampire even as his teeth struck home.

"At the tone the time will be—" said the phone receiver as it fell from his grasp. A single tear slid down his face as he sat there, unable to move. Why the devil couldn't he move?

)0(

"You don't have to pretend you're strong for me, Harley," Anne told him as they crossed the room and sat down together at a table, front and center. "A lot of people fear what they do not understand. It's a perfectly natural reaction. There's something I need to tell you, but perhaps first we'll order the drinks?"

"Good idea," Harley agreed as a waiter came to them. "Hi, do you have any Bloody Mary around here?"

With a chuckle, he replied, "Sir, there's plenty of blood around here. I'll get you one right away. And for you, Miss Salvo?"

"I want sex on the beach," she said with a smirk. "Oh, and I'll take a tequila sunrise, since you're asking."

"You want sex on the beach, eh?" Harley chuckled.

Anne cast him a sultry gaze with her amber eyes and said, "That just might be on the agenda for later, but right now I want to help you in your search for the killer. I happen to know of a few more places around town where vampires like to hang out. I'd like to give them to you, if you will take them. But if I do, you must remember that most of them are not as tame as this."

Amber eyes—a most unusual shade. Where had he seen eyes like that before? Harley wondered.

"This is tame?" he scoffed as a pair of black-clad women began to chase each other around the perimeter of the room. One of them even had fangs in prominent display. They looked remarkably real.

"Yes, Detective Trent," she said seriously. "In this place, most of the people are just pretending to be vampires. But if you go to any of the others, those pretenders won't be there. Or, if they are, they won't be there for long."

"So you're trying to tell me you know of a place with real vampires?" said Harley with a laugh. "That I've got to see."

"Perhaps another day," she conceded. "But tonight is just for us."

Chapter Nine

Though Anne had not told Harley where she was going, he followed her driving directions anyway. He began to wonder just what she was up to when she led him down a long, winding road and they followed it all the way to the end. They continued to drive out onto the beach.

As she got out of the car and let the sand squish between her toes, Harley parked beside her and laughed. "I can't believe you brought me to the beach at midnight. Do you know that we've arrested people for being out on this beach at midnight? It's supposed to be private property."

"Ha! Just tell your underlings it's research work and make them leave," she said with a carefree laugh. Then she yanked her shirt over her head and tossed it on top of the car.

"I don't think they're going to believe my story if we're both completely nude," he pointed out with a grin. His eyes never left her as she playfully removed the rest of her clothes, throwing each piece in his general direction. Harley had to dodge when she threw her shoes as well.

"Aw, can't take a shoe to the gut?" she chuckled.

"I could if I had to," he said, trying not to laugh but failing miserably. Then, completely naked, she stepped up to him with a mischievous grin. Why was that smile so familiar to him? And her eyes—her amber colored eyes. Where had he seen them?

"Come on, Harley," she said as she deftly unbuttoned his shirt. "Time to join the party. You and I are going to go for a swim."

"Are you crazy?" he asked as she pulled his arms free of the shirt, walking all the way in a circle around him to do so. "Do you have any idea how cold that water is?"

"Right now? It's probably about forty-two degrees," she answered. "Why, are you afraid of a little cold water? I never would have thought it of you, Detective."

"I'm not afraid of anything," he said with bravado. "Let's go!"

"Don't you think you might want to take off your pants first?" she chuckled as she tugged at the waistband.

"Um, yeah, that's a good idea," he said sheepishly, and shed the rest of his clothes as quickly as possible. "Okay, now let's go."

With a giggle, Anne grabbed Harley's hand and pulled him along behind her, heading towards the water. She didn't pause when they reached the thundering waves, but simply kept going, pulling him out with her into the shallows.

Harley gasped at the chill, but then he jumped in and went under the surface, emerging with soaking wet hair and hooting triumphantly. "Lord, that's cold!" he said as he wrapped his arms around her neck.

"You look good all wet," Anne told him as she ogled every part she could see. "Almost good enough to eat."

"You look pretty damn good, too, Anne Salvo," he answered, and the two came together, arms pulling each other closer as their lips crushed together, a raging heat swelling between them.

"Oh!" she gasped, and Harley took that opportunity to deepen the kiss. Anne welcomed his tongue in her mouth as though it was the part of her that had always been missing.

"Yes! More!" she breathed.

His hand came up to caress her nipple, while the other he splayed across her back, holding her in place. Then he bent down and took the ridged bit of flesh into his mouth instead. Her hands came up into his hair, holding his head against her insistently as she growled through clenched teeth. She bit her bottom lip as she leaned slightly backward, giving him even better access.

Harley switched his mouth over to the sister breast, thinking it may be jealous of all the attention he was giving to the first one. On the way there he uttered, "These are so perfect, Anne. Your body is perfect. I've never seen a more beautiful woman in my life."

"Hm, I like your pillow talk," she purred.

"What pillow?" Harley chuckled. "We're at the beach."

Anne suddenly grabbed him by the shoulders and tossed him down into the wet sand. A wave crashed over their torsos but did not reach their heads—yet.

"The tide's coming in, you know," Harley mentioned as she ran her tongue down his throat. She grinned up at him when he said this, but made no move to do anything about it.

"I want to taste you, Harley," she said in a sultry whisper.

Her tongue ran lightly over his jugular vein, and Harley gasped at the sensation. Then she was biting him, working her lips up and down and running her tongue over the place her teeth had just been.

About the fourth time she did so, Harley suddenly became aware that the wetness he felt on the area was neither saliva nor seawater.

"What the hell?" he gasped as he tried to sit up. "What are you doing to me?"

"Relax, baby," she cooed in soothing tones. "I'm not going to hurt you. I've got other plans for you. Just lay back and trust me."

"Why are you—uh—why are you biting me

"Shh! All done with that part," she whispered. "Take me, Harley Trent. I want to feel you inside me. Take me right now!"

Aroused more than he had ever been before, Harley wrapped his arms around her waist as he rolled on top of her, moving them so they were further out of the water as he did so.

Without hesitation he slid his hardened cock right inside her pussy and set a slow, languid pace. Anne groaned with each thrust, and she wrapped her legs up around his neck, using them to pull his head toward her own.

"Kiss me, Harley," she said, and he leaned the rest of the way forward and joined his lips to hers. Every time he thrust his pelvis, he thrust his tongue into her mouth as well. Soon both of them were moaning. Their hands gripped and fondled wherever they could find purchase amidst their wild abandon.

Faster and faster. Hotter and hotter. Thrust for thrust. It felt so good Harley thought he would willingly die from the amount of pleasure this woman gave him.

Finally, he burst forth inside of her with every ounce of the passion he'd been building up for over so long. Had it really been over a year since he'd taken a woman? Right this moment, it almost felt like he'd never truly had a woman. Certainly he'd never had one that made him feel like this.

"That was amazing," he told Anne as he lay on top of her, completely spent.

"That was only the beginning," she answered with a smile.

Harley saw blood on the edge of her mouth, and his hand came up to check his neck, coming away with a thick layer of red liquid. Then his head began to spin as Anne continued to watch him, the smile never leaving her lips.

Her eyes turned a golden, glowing shade as her teeth slid out, becoming a pair of fangs. Harley fainted from the shock.

Chapter Ten

Harley awakened still lying on the beach. He was alone. He reached up and checked his neck, and found only a small amount of blood remaining. He began to wonder why it seemed so damned bright outside in the middle of the night.

He made his way to his car and got in, driving himself home more by instinct than anything else. He saw the light flashing on his answering machine as he entered his condo, but he was too tired to care. He went and took a shower, then fell right into his bed.

Fog began to surround him again, but this time the fear was overridden by white-hot desire as

Vivianne lay before him on a sandy beach, smiling up at him with bloody teeth.

Why did this seem so familiar? he wondered as he gazed into her eyes of liquid amber. Amber eyes—where had he seen amber eyes recently?

"Make love to me, Harley Trent," Vivianne said. She'd never called him Harley in any of his dreams before this.

But, gazing upon her naked flesh, his mind remained hazy. He wanted her, wanted her with a need that surpassed all reason. And she was his for the taking.

"Taste me, love," he said to her in a husky whisper. She put his throbbing cock between her sweet red lips, and flayed it with her tongue. Then she set to the task in earnest, and soon he spilled his load right into her mouth.

Now she smiled at him again, and her teeth were covered in contrasting shades of white and red. He thought this should disturb him greatly, yet instead it made him want her even more.

)0(

It was morning. Harley's alarm clock was blaring in his ear, and he rolled groggily over and smacked it across the room. The thing careened across the room and smashed into the wall, shattering into several pieces. Blissful silence met his ears.

As he lay there and awareness returned to him, he tried to remember what had happened the night before, but his mind drew a complete blank. The last thing he could remember was heading for the morgue, but then, nothing.

Sitting up in his bed, he glanced over at his computer screen, which showed a document instead of a screensaver. Thinking this was odd considering the number of hours since he would have last used the machine, Harley furrowed his brow and came to have a look. It was a report of the autopsy he was supposed to view, all neatly typed up.

Although for the life of him he couldn't remember writing it, he wasn't foolish enough to look a gift report in the mouth. Whoever had written it had done him a huge favor, and now he sat and read the thing, familiarizing himself with the content.

About an hour later he took a shower, dressed himself, and emailed the report to himself so he could print it out at work. Well, at least he need not feel guilty over what hour it would be when he got there. It was nothing at all for the Lead Detective to show up sometime after lunch.

More certain than ever about his theory of vampire activities going on, even though he couldn't quite put his finger onto why, Harley decided it was high time he did a little research concerning undead activities in Los Angeles in the past. Not wanting to tell anyone at work about it, he opted to go check in first before heading to the local library and its microfiche room.

As he stepped into the station, Mary caught sight of him and came over with a fresh cup of coffee, plopping it into his hands as she said, "So, how goes the investigation? Any leads?"

"None yet," he said. "Just a whole lot of dead ends."

"You know, boss, there's something different about you," she commented as she gave him the once-over. "You look—I don't know, for lack of a better word—you look a bit more sexy than usual."

"Since when did you think I looked sexy?" Harley inquired with a slight smirk.

"Well, you know I'd never go there, of course," she added quickly. "I don't mix work and pleasure. But still, there's definitely something different about you."

"Maybe it's just because I didn't shave this morning," he suggested.

"Yeah, maybe that's it," she said with a nod. "That must be it."

"Thanks for the coffee, Mary," he said as he turned and headed into his office to retrieve his file.

Once he was done catching up on office work, Harley ducked out the door unnoticed and hopped into his car, intent on going to the library. The sun had come out from behind the clouds, and it seemed more blinding that he remembered.

Then he realized something else. He was driving at breakneck speed, and yet his reflexes were so accurate it seemed almost effortless, even if he had to skirt around other cars. It was almost like playing a full-sized video game.

And it was completely weird.

When he closed and locked the car and headed for the library, he thought he saw a trench coat out of the corner of his eye. His discomfort was clear, but something less clear but more incredible gripped his mind instead.

Perhaps he should follow the trench coat guy and see where he went. Not right now, of course, but maybe when he saw him next time. He was sure there would be a next time—there always was.

"I'd like to use the microfiche room, if I may," he told a librarian. The blatantly homosexual Asian man sauntered along with him to the room in question and unlocked the door.

"Is there anything in particular you want to know, sir?" he inquired.

"Nothing I can't handle on my own," Harley said.

"Too bad, honey," the man replied with a chuckle. "You're missing out if you only ever go solo."

"As a matter of fact, I just got some last night," he commented, and then furrowed his brow. That was right, wasn't it? Hadn't he made love to someone last night? Flashbacks of the time he spent with Anne in the morgue intermittently began to plague his mind as he worked.

Hm, it says here there was some activity in a really old bar near the Hollywood sign called the Bloody Harlot, he thought, trying to think why the name sounded so familiar. Maybe I should try looking there. After I get a few more hours of sleep.

Harley turned off the light on his machine and left the library. At least now he had some kind of a lead to the killer. What he really needed was a lead to what he'd done last night while he was at it.

Chapter Eleven

Harley went straight home and took a long nap. He had intended to sleep only a couple hours, but the next time he opened his eyes the sun had set. Long naps had never been something Harley liked, but he seemed more relaxes and refreshed, and ready to go on the next part of his investigation.

As he slept, he had dreamt again, and the woman in his dreams seemed more familiar than ever. Long blonde hair flowed in sumptuous waves down her back. She probably could sit on it if she wanted to. And those eyes—an odd, amber shade, almost like liquid gold. He had never seen anyone with such unusual eyes.

But then the dream turned once again. He could almost get a look at the face of his attacker, yet somehow the man remained elusive. He was more a representation of a man than a man himself. Harley could never seem to connect the different parts of his face into a recognizable whole. Why couldn't he see his face?

There was no mistaking the sound of that voice, however. It sounded too much like the voice of the strange man in the trench coat.

But how could that be? What connection could there be between a very old city in the past and this trench-coated figure here in the present? None of it made any sense.

He knew it would be stupid to go into a bar alone looking like a cop, so he fumbled through his closets looking for a less formidable outfit to wear. What did one wear to fit in among a bunch of vampires in some bar, anyway?

He settled on all black clothes. As an afterthought, he even put a little gel in his hair and gave it a bit if a spike. If only the Sergeant could see his new Lead Detective now!

He hopped into his sleek black sedan and revved it up, then backed out just as the man in the trench coat rounded the corner. "Missed me for once, didn't you?" he scoffed, then commenced to driving down the road.

Not too much later, Harley looked with annoyance in his rearview mirror at a strobing light. He turned the car off and patiently waited for the rookie to approach.

"License and registration, please," he said.

"Is there a problem, officer?" Harley asked as he gave the man his wallet. It contained his badge and credentials as well as his identification.

"Detective Trent? I didn't recognize you in that get-up," he said as he gave the wallet right back. "So, did you know you're driving without any headlights, sir?"

"Am I?" he asked, surprised. He glanced down and saw the man was right. "Well I'll be. I never even noticed a difference."

"Well, sir, you might want to turn those on."

"Yes, thank you, officer. I'll do that right away," he agreed, turning the knob in question into the 'on' position. "Good eye, son. Keep up the good work."

"Thanks, Detective," he replied, giving Harley a salute.

As he watched the young man go, Harley shook his head in consternation. "What the devil has gotten into me?" he muttered as he turned the ignition on again.

He made it to the Bloody Harlot in no time, and found it to be every bit as run down and decadent as his imagination had allowed him to believe. He couldn't believe how many people in Los Angeles really wanted to be vampires.

Off in one corner, he spotted a man in a trench coat watching him. Their eyes met, and the man beckoned him to approach. As he took the bar stool beside the other man's a spark of recognition had his nerves roiling. This was the man who had been stalking him lately, he was certain of it.

"Detective Trent, you're full of surprises," the man said with an indulgent smile. "I never would have thought you'd be stupid enough to come in a place like this on your own."

"Why does this place seem familiar?" Harley wanted to know.

"Because you've been here before, of course," he explained. "My name is Lazzo Amakiir, at your service. What brings you to this place, might I inquire?"

"Curiosity?" Harley answered uncertainly.

"That I can believe," he agreed. "But you were spotted here last night with a beautiful woman. One would think your curiosity had been sated by now."

"I—I was here last night?" Harley inquired. "With a woman? What did she look like? I can't remember a thing about last night."

"Anne Salvo is a beautiful woman," Lazzo commented. "Only a man who cared little for such things would have forgotten something like that."

"No, I don't remember her," Harley admitted. "I can't remember being here, either.
Although when I look around it feels quite familiar somehow."

"That is as it should be," he explained. "The loss of memory is only a temporary thing, Mr. Trent. But it usually follows the bite of a vampire who wishes to make you its thrall. Do you remember being bitten last night, Detective?"

Harley slid a hand over the set of puncture wounds he'd found on his neck that morning but had not bothered to examine yet. There appeared to be four of them.

"I think maybe I was bitten," he answered.

"Then I am too late," Lazzo said solemnly. "I was sent here to ensure your safety during the matters which are upcoming."

"I'm not at all certain which matters you mean," Harley commented as he looked the man in his eyes. Unlike the black pools he'd seen before, they were a simple shade of blue.

"That's very refreshing," said Lazzo. "So, would you like to try the beach out with someone who really knows how to please a man?"

"Excuse me?"

"Come on, Trent, don't be coy," he smirked. "I want to see just how nice it really was."

"You're crazy," Harley informed him. "I really don't swing that way."

"You used to," he commented wryly. "In a former life."

"How would you know?" Harley scoffed.

"I can read your aura," Lazzo explained. "If you want to have a power as great as mine, Detective, you're going to have to earn it, plain and simple. I know what it is you truly seek. You wake every morning in a cold sweat, trying to make sense of it all, yet still you have not found the key to explain your dreams. I may be able to help you, if you will allow me."

"No, you're mistaken," Harley lied. "All I want is to solve this case."

"If that was all you wanted, fate never would have brought you here," Lazzo insisted. "Still, I want to help you with the case as well. The killer is making the rest of our kind look much worse than we truly are, and he must be stopped. Will you accept the help I offer?"

"Help, yes," Harley said, then leaned in closer to add. "Anything more than that, no."

"Well then, I shall just have to take what I can get."

Chapter Twelve

"What is this place?" Harley asked Lazzo as the pair of them got out of his car.

Stepping around to the front of the car to join him as they walked towards a very old castle, Lazzo replied, "This is the home of one of the most feared vampires in the city. Whatever preconceived notions you have of vampires should be left outside these walls, because you're in for a bit of a culture shock, Detective Trent."

"You're seriously going to tell me that this place belongs to a vampire?" Harley scoffed. Looking at the stones as they reached the front door, he added, "It sure looks like it could. But how did an old castle get here?"

"It was moved here, stone by stone, by servants of Demetrius—the vampire you are about to meet," Lazzo explained. "Be careful in this place, my friend. Most of the people in here would rather eat you than greet you."

"Are they all vampires?"

"Not all," Lazzo conceded. "Some of them are worse."

"Great, you just brought me here to slaughter, didn't you?" Harley grumbled. "That just figures."

"Don't worry, Harley, none of them will touch you while you are under my protection," he reassured him, grasping his shoulder briefly and giving it a squeeze. "They may get the impression that I have a reason to protect you, though. It would be best if you allowed them to believe it, if you take my meaning."

"You mean pretend that I'm your lover?" asked Harley with distaste.

"At least long enough to get what you came here for," Lazzo said. "And remember, vampires can be very cunning. There are many intrigues going on around here. It is best for you not to inadvertently entangle yourself in any of them. I will try my best to guide you, but still you must be wary."

"I'll do my best," Harley agreed, and then they went through the huge double doors and stepped down into the darkened Great Hall.

After his eyes became more accustomed to the sudden lack of light, Harley began to look around the huge room curiously. In one half of the area, they'd set up a large dance floor. A real band was on a stage playing a waltz, and the dancers held each other and whirled about accordingly.

None of them looked anything like what he'd expected. They looked like perfectly normal humans. No protruding fangs, no hissing, no turning into bats. It looked like a simple dance party, with the people there having a really good time.

He had been about to lose interest in them completely until he spotted Anne Salvo dancing among them. His eyes drank her in, and in that moment he came to realize what he hadn't seen before this. Anne was the woman in his dreams. And if she was here, that also meant that she must be one of them. A vampire.

Harley was somewhat surprised by his response to this bit of news. He would have thought learning this truth would put him off completely, making him never want to speak to the beautiful woman again. But instead, he was overcome by a deep longing to go over there and take her into his arms. Had she not vowed that she would look until she found him again?

Before he could speculate much more on this, and before he could even wonder how come he'd spent the whole day trying to remember what he'd done the night before, but just one look at Anne brought everything back into sharp clarity, she suddenly looked directly at him. Her amber eyes flashed with momentary interest, and then she caught sight of his companion and scowled.

Sauntering over to the pair of them, she smiled sweetly as she inquired, "Hello, Detective Trent. I had no idea that you and Lazzo knew one another."

"We've only just met," Harley explained. "I told him I had an interest in learning more about the vampire culture hidden within our city, and he obligingly brought me here."

"That was—unwise, was it not, Lazzo?" she said, and her golden eyes flashed like those of a cat in the darkness. Harley was mesmerized by those eyes, as before, but this time he did not allow himself to be so easily taken in.

"Will you dance with me, Detective?" Anne asked as she slid a hand around his arm, tugging gently.

"Of course I will, Anne," he agreed with a smile. "I'll dance with you anytime you like."

While they were out on the dance floor, Lazzo wandered about the room speaking with people here and there. He approached a large, tawny-haired man and as they spoke, the pair of them looked directly over to Harley.

"Who is that man?" Harley asked Anne.

Glancing over, she looked back at him and said, "That is no man, Harley. That is the pack leader here in Los Angeles. No matter where or how we were made, every vampire here must answer to him. It's kind of like we're the mob and he's the Don."

"So you admit that you're a vampire?" he inquired.

"I would have thought you'd noticed that by now," she chuckled, sliding a couple fingers over the bite mark she'd recently administered.

"You did some kind of a memory erase on me, didn't you?"

"No, it is a result of the bite," she explained. "I could not shield you from that effect, no matter what. I am glad to see that you have regained your mind as quickly as you have. It is a very promising omen."

"Promising?" he repeated. "In what way, promising?"

"If you were to be bitten two more times, you would be one of us," she explained.

"Wait, you mean if any vampires bite me, I'll be turned?"

"No, love," she said, drawing him closer so she could speak in his ear. "The same vampire must bite you all three times. If another bites you, it could kill you. So do have a care, won't you?"

"And what if I don't want to become a vampire?" Harley wanted to know.

"I will not turn you against your will," she said. "But do not think that means I wouldn't try to change your will to match mine."

"Lazzo told me vampires are really into intrigue," Harley said with a smirk. "But I'm beginning to think you are the most intriguing of them all."

Chapter Thirteen

While they were still dancing, Harley glanced around the room as a cheer went up among the others. Someone had been putting a red liquid in all their cups, and now they began to drink it. He didn't really want to think about where that liquid had come from.

Anne, seeing the look on his face, turned his head back so she could look into his eyes. "Harley, it's all right. You don't have to drink. But if you do, there can be no turning back. If you drink, it shows your willingness to join our little gang. There are only two types of members in it, Harley. The vampires, and humans who willingly give blood when it is needed."

"You don't kill your humans?" he asked.

"No, we use them like cows, in a way," she said. "Until they decide to turn, the humans are free to come and go at will. Many of them take care of our daytime business so we don't have to do it ourselves. But all of them give blood at least twice in a week."

"Sounds like you've got it all planned out," he answered with a snort.

"It is better this way," she said. "If the vampires were left to feed as they used to, you would have a lot more murders to wade through in that job of yours."

"But one of them is not playing by your rules," Harley pointed out.

"Harley, you can still keep your job if you change," she told him as she grabbed a glass from the tray of a passing waiter. Harley cringed slightly as she drank from it.

"I—I don't know, Anne," he hedged. "It's just such a big decision to make. I'm somewhat frightened by the idea, truth be told."

Anne didn't say another word. Instead, she pulled his head down to hers and kissed him. Liquid gushed from her mouth into his, and Harley's head began to spin wildly. He held fast to Anne's shoulders, filled with a heady desire for both more of the liquid and more of her.

"Come, Harley," she whispered as she led him toward the newel staircase at the back of the hall. Together they climbed up to the top and down a corridor. Anne did not stop until they reached the very last door. When she opened it, they walked into the most sumptuous bedroom he'd ever seen.

"What are we doing in here?" he asked with an amused smirk.

"Anything we like," she explained. "No one will disturb us in this chamber."

"Do you know what I'd like?" he inquired.

"I have a pretty good idea," she told him with a grin. She reached back and deftly undid the zipper of her gown. She let it fall to the floor and stepped neatly out of it. Her bra and panties soon joined the gown. The high heels she left on.

The whole time she unclothed herself all Harley could do was stare. How could any woman be so exquisite? She was the most beautiful creature he's ever seen—and she knew it.

"Take off your clothes, Detective Harley Trent," she said on a whisper. "I want to taste you."

"But Anne, I thought that you biting me would make me turn," he pointed out.

"Not yet, it wouldn't," she reassured him. "It usually happens on the third bite."

"Anne, how often do vampires need blood?" he wanted to know.

"A least once a week if they wish to remain civilized," she said. "Unfortunately, if they do not partake during that timeframe, they will go hunt down some prey to feed the hunger they can never avoid."

"If—"

"Do you always ask so many questions when a naked woman who is hot after your body stands before you?" she inquired, smirking.

Harley took the hint. When he kissed her, it was like the whole world had exploded into sensual pleasure. His desire skyrocketed and careened off the walls, then dropped ten anvils on his head for good measure.

"Give in to it, Harley," she instructed. "I can help you."

Wordlessly, Harley lifted Anne into his arms and lay her on the furs covering the bed. Then he stepped back long enough to remove his clothes also.

"You are so beautiful," he whispered as he lay down beside her on the bed. "I think you are the only woman I've ever loved. Isn't that crazy?"

"Not crazy at all," she said with a smile.

Harley's hands came up to massage her breasts, and Anne groaned with pleasure. When he'd finished with them he next moved a bit further down, resting his head between her legs.

Anne giggled. "What are you doing?"

"I want to taste you," he answered wickedly, and nipped her thigh before putting his words into action. He may as well have been lapping at honey, he enjoyed her taste so much. "Damn, even this part of you is perfect."

The words combined with the intimate touch combined were too much for her. Anne felt herself letting go. She felt her fangs beginning to sprout, but she did not want him to stop. She had waited almost five hundred years to reunite with this man's soul. She wanted to possess him, but only if he was willing to let her.

"Make love to me, Harley," she pleaded. "I want you inside me."

Harley came back up and softly kissed her lips before he plunged right in. The two of them pounded into each other in afrenzy, vocalizing their pleasures wherever it seemed appropriate.

Anne bit him just as their climax hit. This, of course, made Harley so dizzy he passed out, just as he'd done before. But this time, she woke him up again.

"Harley," she chided. "I'm not nearly done with you."

Grinning, Harley said, "He may need a bit of incentive if you want him again."

With her jewel-bright eyes glinting in the darkness, Anne's gaze went from his face down to the 'he' in question. "You're not afraid I'll bite?" she teased.

"I don't think that's the spot you'd bite, is it?"

"Harley, don't you know? There's more than one main vein in the human body," she teased him. "Do you trust me?"

"Always," he answered truthfully.

Anne dipped her head down between his thighs and took his cock into her mouth, sucking it to life. Then she moved up and mounted him, saying, "I want to ride you and ride you and ride you."

"I've heard that before," he whispered.

"I know," she answered sweetly, and then she put her words into action.

Chapter Fourteen

The next day Harley scooted out of the empty bed in the strange castle with no idea how he'd gotten there. Bright sunlight streamed in through the window, making his eyes hurt and his flesh tingle. He tried very hard to recall how he'd come to be here, but he couldn't put two thoughts together inside his mind.

Locating his clothes, Harley dressed himself and then opened the door a crack to peek outside. Seeing no one in the hall, he swiftly ran down the corridor to the newel staircase he discovered on the far end. He vaguely remembered seeing it once before.

Down the circular staircase he descended, right into the great hall. Compared to the party he seemed to recall from the night before, the place seemed uninvitingly dead. He wanted to get out of there as soon as possible.

"Good morning," said a smooth male voice.

Harley turned just as he reached the door to answer. It would be rude not to, even by the standards of the undead. "Hello—uh—good morning to you, too."

"No doubt you know who I am?" inquired the tawny-haired vampire as he looked him over like a cat would look at its toy mouse. Harley had the distinct feeling he wanted to pounce.

"Yes, you're the man in charge," he commented as he nervously rubbed at the back of his neck. "But I don't believe I caught your name."

"I am Demetrius Nosandre," he said with a graceful bow. "I was made well over a thousand years ago, and I am the oldest vampire in this city. All the vampires in this area must obey me without question. You, too, will be expected to comply. But we can discuss that more tonight. There will be another party, and I would very much like you to attend."

"Mr. Demetrius—sir—I don't remember what you're talking about," he replied. "How did I get here to begin with? Why am I still here? How are you able to be awake during the daylight?"

"Ah, yes, she must have bitten you again," he chuckled. "The mind is always a bit addled just after a good—biting. This place is my home, Castle Nosandre. And do not worry about your memory. It will return to you in due time."

"Uh, thanks?" Harley replied uncertainly.

"Now go, Detective," he said as he turned away. "Return to me tonight."

Harley was watching the vampire as he moved away when he noticed something odd. A small portion of the cloak he was wearing appeared to be missing. Just the right size to match the piece he'd found in the penthouse apartment recently.

"I look forward to it," he commented, hiding his reaction as best he could. Then he too turned, and exited the building.

If he'd thought his reflexes were lightning fast yesterday, he didn't know what he was talking about. This time he sped through town so fast and so smooth he could have broken the sound barrier without batting an eye. It put him very much in the mood to go buy himself a better car.

Harley had originally decided to return to the library to see if he could find any information about Demetrius, but found that he was feeling somewhat drained. The sun was annoyingly hot, and he had to put on his shades just to tolerate it.

Still, he needed to follow the new lead, so he forced himself to stop off for an hour or so at the very least. As he entered the small, two story building the man from before approached with a smile.

"Microfiche again?" he asked.

"Yes, please," Harley answered as he removed his sun glasses and put them in his pocket for safe keeping.

"You look like you had a rough night," the man commented with a smirk. "Out getting some more, were you?"

"Oh, yeah," Harley commented with a wink.

"Lucky guy," he chortled as he went away again.

There were several articles about vampire cults all over the country that had once been headed up by "a mysterious figure who refused to be interviewed", and one very interesting article concerning imported castles.

This one in particular had been rebuilt where it stood two hundred years ago. Had Demetrius been living there all that time, he wondered. Checking out the article, he could easily recognize the structure he had just emerged from not even two hours earlier.

Demetrius had been right about his memories returning. They'd done so much sooner this time. Remembering the woman who worked in the morgue's name was Anne Salvo, he decided he ought to look up any information he could get on her as well. Somehow, even though he could not think why, he just knew she was significant.

Apparently during the sixties the woman was at a sit-in protesting the Vietnam war, and she'd also been spotted in the seventies at a flag burning, but other than that she checked out okay.

Except, of course, for the fact that the date of birth had to be phony. If she'd really been born in sixty-two, she would only have been a small child in the sixties. Didn't anyone else ever read these things?

Making print-outs of everything he had just discovered, Harley rolled them up and slipped them into his briefcase, then left the library with a wave to the librarian.

"Good luck tonight, tiger!" the man called with a grin.

"You too, buddy," Harley answered. Then he decided to go home and sleep away a few hours as he waited for night to fall.

Anne Salvo came to him in his dreams. He couldn't decide if he was making up what happened, or if this dream was somehow linked to reality.

"Take me, Harley," she said as she shed her clothing within a second. "I need you to be with me. Be with me now."

"I love you," Harley whispered against her lips. "But how do I know what part of all this is real, and what part is fantasy?"

"Be with me forever, Harley," she pleaded as he sank his shaft inside her. "All it takes is one little bite. And then you'll get to be immortal again."

Harley came then, and the climax awakened him before he could respond.

Be with her forever? Become immortal again? He didn't know if he was ready to do that. Did he really want to become like her? Like she believed he'd been once before—a vampire? A dark creature of the night who was forever hungering, seeking the blood of others to continue his unending existence?

But, if he was truly immortal in the past, then how could that body have died? How could a man be immortal if he died? Perhaps because his soul had not died? It was all so confusing, and he didn't understand it at all. Maybe his brain was still too fogged over to understand.

With a heavy sigh, Harley rolled over onto his side and tried to sleep a while longer, willing the sweet Miss Salvo to still be in his dreams

Chapter Fifteen

Even though he felt that returning to the ancient vampire and his strange old castle was a foolish idea at best, Harley still found himself arriving there at sunset. He shook his head in consternation as he wondered what he must be thinking.

You're just thinking with your dick, he told himself as he headed inside. And that's a really bad idea. You need to get your head back into the game if you want to catch the killer, otherwise he may just catch you.

Entering the Great Hall, Harley looked around, hoping to see a familiar face. Preferably Anne's face, since that was the real reason he'd come back. But he didn't see even one person he knew, so he just stood near the door, feeling more foolish than ever.

As he observed the others in the room, he finally saw Demetrius standing off to one side, observing him. Their eyes met and held, but then suddenly the vampire was gone.

"Come, Detective Trent, we are all gathering at the beach for our party tonight," said Demetrius as he came up behind Harley and laid a hand on his back. "I will drive you there in your car."

"Vampires can drive?" Harley asked in surprise as he turned to look at him.

"Of course we can drive," he said with a short laugh. "And, we can also go out in the daylight despite the fact it causes us such discomfort. Much of what you have been told about vampires is either exaggerated or just plain wrong."

"I can believe that," Harley said with a slight smile. "People are really good at making mountains out of mole hills. And at calling something evil just because they don't understand it."

"You must have a great many questions at this point, do you not?" he asked as they walked out to his poorly parked vehicle. "If you want to know anything at all, you need only ask and I shall endeavor to answer." Harley did not say anything until they were both seated in his car and the vampire was on the road. "Why so quiet, Detective?"

"Just collecting my thoughts," Harley told him. "I would have thought that Anne would be the one to teach me about being a vampire, if I even decide to be one."

"Anne means well, but she is too soft-hearted," Demetrius excused her. "There are aspects of this life that she would like to deny."

"So you don't think a vampire should be soft-hearted?" Harley chuckled.

"It is not a very helpful trait in someone who by their very nature must feed off of others in order to survive," he said with an indulgent smirk. "Only imagine a soft-hearted alligator, and you will understand what I mean. If he does not kill something else, he will die of starvation. It is worse for a vampire, however, for if we do not feed regularly, we don't die, we lose ourselves to that need. I'm surprised Anne has lasted as long as she has, truth be told."

"And how long is that, exactly?" Harley asked curiously.

"That is a question you must ask her for yourself," Demetrius told him. "A vampire's past is a very personal matter. I would not willingly divulge mine to just anyone, and with good reason. But, I can tell you this—I was already a vampire in the times of the Christ, and also was among the guards who came to take him away. This is not something I care to brag about, for we were ordered to brutalize a man whose only crime was using his influence and abilities to help others. That was when I learned a simple truth. If one simply ceases to care, they are capable of doing anything they put their minds to. No matter what it might be."

"And every vampire ceases to care?"

"No, many of them do not embrace my ideal," he conceded. "But they would be far better off if they did."

"So you would know which of them might be a cold-blooded killer who ripped open the throats of eight people?" Harley inquired with venom in his tone.

"Detective, the vampires I associate with are much more civilized than that," he said smoothly. "If I knew one of them was responsible, I'd rip their throats open in a similar manner."

"Really?" he asked. "And if you did, wouldn't the victim of your cruel punishment simply regenerate?"

Demetrius laughed. "It's not that simple, Detective. You see, although we can regenerate it would take years to recover from an injury like that one."

"So in effect, we'd have another serial killing spree, just a few years later?" Harley said. "That hardly sounds like an effective strategy."

Demetrius turned onto a long, dark road as he chuckled again. "It's probably more effective than you arresting and incarcerating a vampire who would then be able to feed off and maybe even convert the whole inmate population. Only image the carnage that would cause."

"Can't you drive a wooden stake into his heart?" Harley asked. "That is a way to end them longer, but as you know more than anyone else, that would not stop them forever," he said. "His soul would return again."

"Maybe, but would that soul always have a drive to kill?"

"Don't you, Detective?" Demetrius turned his question around.

Harley sat there a moment, contemplating. "Yes, I suppose I do," he said softly. "However, I've managed to suppress it."

"That's good," he said as they pulled to a stop. "Here we are. Feel free to mingle, have fun, do as you wish. Tonight is a celebration of sorts. The moon is at its darkest."

"You celebrate a dark moon?" Harley asked. "Why would you do that?"

"In ancient times the darkest hour was when the werewolves were at their weakest, and vampires could kill them." he said. "It's a brutal tradition to celebrate, but no more brutal some of the other traditions the mortals follow."

"What holiday do we have that celebrates killing?" Harley wanted to know.

"Veteran's Day, for one," he said. "Don't get me wrong, I find it wise to remember the dead, but one would be better off not to celebrate war."

"And yet the tradition you describe does the same thing," said Harley with a smug grin. "You're celebrating the war between vampires and werewolves."

"It's not the same," he said. "Werewolves kill indiscriminately, and do not care what happens as a result of their rampaging. If they wish to act like beasts instead of men, they should be treated as such."

"So you don't believe in equal rights for all immortals?"

With a wry grin, Demetrius got out of the car, then bent his head in to say, "I believe everyone has a right to my opinion, whether they want it or not."

Harley shook his head as he followed him out into the sand.

Chapter Sixteen

Harley and Demetrius parted company soon after their arrival at the same beach Anne had brought him to before. Although he spotted Lazzo, he decided not to join him since he was obviously trying to gain the attention of a fellow male vampire who seemed to like the idea immensely. He wanted no part in that.

All he really wanted, of course, was to find Anne. He milled slowly through the crowd looking for her silvery-blonde mane, but after an hour of hunting he determined she most definitely was not there.

With an inward sigh, he tried to enjoy himself without her. He'd always been really terrible at parties. While other people would laugh and play and get drunk, he'd only ever learned to accomplish the getting drunk part. He thought about it for a while, and then moved over to the keg and got himself a pint-sized cup of cider.

The coolness of the chilled beverage soothed his throat, while the afterbite told him this was some mighty powerful stuff. Two or three pints of this, and he would be a complete mess.

However, since he was currently surrounded by unfamiliar vampire types, he tended to think that losing himself to the oblivion of drink was a bad idea. He might be the next drained body on the news, he thought with a shudder.

That made him wonder how he could even be here. Did he want this kind of life? Did he want to be the one doing the draining instead of the one searching for the killer? Was the delectable Anne Salvo enough of an incentive to become that which he most vehemently abhorred?

But even as he allowed the idea that he abhorred these people enter his mind, he pushed it out again with equal vehemence. Just as Anne had said, Harley had always been fascinated by death.

He feared death, truth be told. She was offering him a way to cheat death, if he were to turn. He could live a life as a stronger being, become a great force for good or ill, the choice was his to make.

When he heard the announcement that the refreshments had arrived, Harley circumspectly wandered away from the group. This was the part of the whole situation he could not stomach.

Even though the meal had probably been willingly provided, he didn't know if he'd ever be able to stomach something as disgusting as drinking another person's blood.

Really, how did they know where the human who provided it had been? Did they give the donors a pop quiz as to their eating habits, drug habits, and sex habits before they syphoned him, or what?

Harley stopped by his car to toss in his socks and shoes, and then ambled along the beach barefoot for a while. When he spotted a lone female figure walking along just inside the water, he knew instantly it was Anne. Perhaps she was no fan of large gatherings either.

"Hello, beautiful," he said as she reached him.

Rather than answer, she pulled him to her for a kiss instead. And oh, what a kiss it was. Harley could not ignore its intensity or its duration. A most carnal need arose within him, and she stoked it with her kisses.

"Anne," he whispered urgently against her lips. "I don't know if I'm ready to—"

"Shh, don't worry," she told him. "I won't turn you unless you ask me to. It would be cruel to do so."

"All right," he agreed.

"This beach seems destined to provide us with a surface for lovemaking," Anne teased him as his hands brushed over her erect nipples. "Take me, Harley. Take me now."

Harley tossed her down into the sand and she rolled over and yanked him down on top of her.

They kissed each other with wild abandon, wanting and taking, neither in control but both in accord. Hands sought and found, clothes came off and were discarded carelessly to wherever they might fall, and then he was deep inside her.

Anne clung to Harley, both arms around his waist and hands periodically exploring his buttocks. They made enough noise to wake the dead, or at least alert the undead to their presence. Luckily, none of the vampires showed up to view the spectacular show they put on.

Her mouth came down onto his throat, and her tongue ran along the scars of the previous bites she'd given him. Harley paused for a moment, wondering if she was thinking to bite him after all, but she did not.

"Harley, please!" she hissed, pulling him closer than ever. "Please make me come.!"

With a grin, Harley slammed into her harder than ever. Their voices rang out into the night, echoing all around them. When both of them were sated, they just laid there on the beach, holding hands and staring up at the stars.

Thoughts of the case threatened to intrude on the moment, but Harley tamped them down resolutely. Tonight was not about murders and killers and such, it was about Anne. He really wanted to be with her, really needed to be with her, and yet he feared that the only way he could was to become like her.

Would he be able to stomach being a vampire? he asked himself yet again. Would he be able to drink the blood of other people just to sustain himself?

All moralistic concerns aside, he wondered what would become of him if he did so. Eventually he would have to pretend to die in this life, and relocate. That was the pattern Demetrius followed, and Anne as well. The microfiche never lied.

It was a rather depressing thought, that he'd have to leave his job, his friends, and everything he knew at some point. But he would be alive, and he would be with Anne. He just didn't know what to do.

"What are you thinking about, Harley?" Anne asked as she buried her face against his chest.

"I'm thinking about reality, and my place within it," he admitted. "Silly man, it's really quite simple," she said. "If you just accept reality, then it can be kind. It does no good to fight against it, because if it's really reality it's going to happen regardless."

"Boy, does that sound remarkably like a greeting card," he teased her.

"How do you mean?" she asked, confused..

"Well, just the idea, really," he answered, nuzzling her hair with his chin. "To accept that reality cannot be changed. But in my world, I see reality as ever-changing. We make our own destinies, Anne. I just don't know yet what mine will be."

"Give it time," she said sleepily. "Everything that leaves us always returns eventually."

Then the pair drifted off to sleep together. In the morning, Harley woke alone. He got into his car and drove home, more than ready to crash in his bed when he got there.

Chapter Seventeen

Del Brucco drove up to the large brownstone condominiums where his best friend and recently promoted co-worker lived. He had tried to call Harley more times than he cared to remember over the last couple of days, and had not received even one call in return. He didn't even answer when Del texted him.

He was beginning to think that something was terribly wrong.

But that was not the only reason he had for paying Harley a visit. It was also vitally important to inform him that yet another killing had occurred—if he was even alive to tell.

Frank Jefferson's death had hit everyone on the team pretty hard. Over the last twenty-four hours he'd gotten no sleep whatsoever, for everyone on the team had been hard at work looking for leads that would lead them to whoever—or whatever—had taken the life of a man they'd all come to love and respect.

He was certain that Harley was likely to take that death the hardest of them all. Jefferson was his mentor, his colleague, and his best friend in a way Del could never be.

While he and Harley had known each other since just after high school, when they'd both joined the force, it was Frank Jefferson who had inspired him to choose his career path as a detective. He looked up to the man like the father he never really had.

He needed to be told.

Since Del knew the combination to the building's outer door, he simply let himself in. The doorman looked up and waved at him in recognition, not bothering to ask where he was going. Del waved back as he continued to walk toward the elevator.

Several minutes ticked by waiting for the damned elevator to arrive. Del impatiently got in and pushed the five button. The doors clicked shut, sounds of movement accosted his ears above the quiet music in the background, and then the doors slid open again. He didn't bother to knock on Harley's door, but let himself inside instead.

"Harley?" he called as he headed for the bedroom. "Hey, Harley? Are you still alive back here?"

He found Harley sprawled across the bed as though he'd crashed there and had not taken a moment to pull the covers up over him. He was lying there in a pool of drool, assend up in the air, and arms tucked underneath himself in a manner that was sure to cut off his circulation.

Wondering if he'd been drinking, Del sniffed the air near him experimentally. Not unless the alcohol had no odor, he concluded.

"Wake up, Harley," he said, shaking him. "Wake up, you sorry excuse for an officer. Where the hell have you been all week?"

Harley barely even twitched a muscle. Del was halfway contemplating the idea of checking him for a pulse. Then, quite suddenly, the man was wide awake. He rolled over and glared at Del irritably.

"What the heck did you wake me up for?" he demanded hotly.

"Just where the hell have you been?" Del wanted to know. "Even if you are the Lead Detective that doesn't give you a right to not check in. How can you solve the case if you don't even have all the facts?"

"Sorry, Del," he said, giving his friend's hand an apologetic squeeze. "I've been—chasing down a lead, I guess you'd say. I haven't gotten much sleep, either, if you don't mind."

"I do mind—sir," he said. "I have something very important to tell you. Something I've wanted to tell you for a couple days now."

"What is it now," Harley grumbled. "There's been another killing, hasn't there?"

"I'm afraid so," said Del gravely. "The killer has struck pretty close to home this time. I think he may be trying to throw it in our faces that we still haven't caught him."

"Why?" Harley asked as he sat up. "Who did he kill this time?"

"Frank Jefferson," Del told him gravely.

"What? Why the hell would anybody do that?" Harley gasped, his stomach lurching. "He can't have tasted very good at his age—"

"Tasted good?" Del scoffed. "Please don't tell me you've been chasing after vampires all this time, because if you do, I'm having you committed once and for all."

"I have been," he told him stubbornly. "And do you know what I found out? They're real, Del. They are as real as you or me or—well, anybody, for that matter. In fact, they could be anybody you know. One of them could even be me, and you wouldn't know it."

"Oh, so now you're a vampire?" Del asked in disgust.

"No, not yet," he admitted as he unconsciously rubbed at his bite marks. "I haven't made the final choice to become one. But Del, you should really come with me and see for yourself. I could use a little collaboration."

"The only place you're going right now is down to the precinct so we can process Frank's death properly. He's been on ice waiting for you for three days already. The Lead Detective has to give the go-ahead on all cases. You know that."

"Yes, of course I know," he grumbled. "I was briefed on the job when I took it. But maybe tonight you could—"

"I have plans of my own tonight," Del cut him off. "Maybe you should come with me, since this is right up your alley. I got a tip that there's a cult of vampire wannabes who have been terrorizing people near the shore.

Personally, I want to chase after vampires as much as I want to jump out of a perfectly good airplane, but this could lead us towards that theory of yours, you know?"

Harley held back a sigh and mentally kicked Del in the head half a dozen times. He'd just gotten done telling him that there were really vampires in the city, and he'd even been bold enough to tell him he was on the verge of becoming one, and all he wanted to do was go scare up some fake ones? What was it going to take to get him to believe all of this?

He took the set of clothes that Del got out for him and put them on, and then the two each took a car and headed back to the police station.

Chapter Eighteen

"Lord, we are dealing with one sick bastard. Why did he have to cut Jefferson up so much when he must have been dead after the first two or three blows?" said Harley to Del as the two finally got out of the briefing room.

"Would you like me to go down to the morgue with you?" asked Del sympathetically as he saw the direction of Harley's gaze. "I know you have to go."

"Standard procedure," Harley commented. He wondered if Anne had found it difficult to process a man she'd been working with as yet another stiff.

Did vampires still have feelings like guilt or remorse or sorrow?

"Let's go," he said, not bothering to tell Del they were about to meet a vampire. He probably wouldn't believe him anyway.

The receptionist looked up with a smile as the two men walked in.

"Good afternoon, Detective Trent," she said. "Ms. Salvo is expecting you. And I see you've brought a friend. Sir, if you're going into the morgue you need to sign in. Thanks."

After signing, Del gave the clipboard back, and she read his name. "Del Brucco, eh? I've heard your name before somewhere."

"I hope so, I've been on the force fifteen years," he answered with a teasing snort.

"Del, flirt on your own time, will you?" Harley grumbled as he headed for the door he'd entered the last time he was here.

"Maybe I will," he answered as he followed him, then he turned back long enough to wink at her before they stepped inside.

Anne was just finishing up with another body and then she had the technicians bring out Frank for his autopsy. "You gentlemen can wait outside, if you like," she said, mostly for Del's benefit.

"Yeah, that might be a good idea," he agreed, grinning at Harley.

"You go flirt with her, I'll stay here and flirt with this one," Harley said with a wink.

"Something tells me you've flirted with this one before," Del said as he looked Anne over appreciatively.

"That's one of this job's perks," Harley said. "You get to meet the most beautiful woman in the world."

"Harley, stop," Anne said with a blush.

"Jefferson is ready when you are, ma'am," the technician announced as he and his partner left the room.

"Thanks," Anne called after them.

"That's my cue to exit, stage right," Del commented, giving the two of them a wink.

After Del was gone, Harley asked, "Where did you disappear to last night?"

"Back to my coffin, of course," she teased him.

"You don't seriously have to sleep in a coffin, do you?" Harley asked with a worried tone.

"Of course not, Detective," she told him. "That's just a silly folk tale to keep us vampire children in line."

"Funny," he said playfully as he grabbed some gloves and proceeded to assist her without being asked this time. "Are there actually vampire children?"

"No one can be turned until they reach puberty," she said. "However, yes, vampires do have the ability to produce offspring, and I was the offspring of a vampire couple. I grew up knowing that I would be turned once I reached sixteen."

"And were you okay with that?"

"Yes," she answered. "To me, it seemed perfectly natural, because I was born to it."

"So, when did you have to start drinking blood, not until you turned?" he asked.

"It was not necessary until then, but I was given blood in my sippy cup, so to speak," she explained. "I suppose that is why I don't mind this line of work. Now stop talking, I need to record observations and don't want this discussion on the tape."

Harley chuckled. "Yeah, I could see where that would be undesirable."

"I have really missed your sense of humor," she mentioned as she pulled the mask over her face.

"Sorry about that," he answered sincerely. "And if you turn me, will I still have it?"

"If it can survive several centuries worth of reincarnations, I'm pretty sure it will withstand something as simple as a turning."

"Simple?" he scoffed. "You think it's simple to become immortal, to know you'll have to deceive friends and family, to know that eventually you'll have to either tell them the truth or pretend to die? I can't think how that's simple."

"I suppose from the viewpoint you describe it's not so simple," she admitted. "Now shut up already, so I can get out of here sometime today."

"Yes, ma'am," Harley chuckled, and did as he was told.

Chapter Nineteen

"So, where's your pretend vampire suspect?" Harley asked Del after they'd left the two women behind and headed for their cars. "We may as well round him up for questioning."

"His name is Erick Strumpkull, but he goes by the handle 'Blaze'. He's part owner of a bar called "Vampire's Dive", where most of the clients dress like vampires and pretend to bite each other. It's a really cheesy place."

"I can imagine," Harley said wryly.

"I was thinking we'd fit in better if we dressed up like vampires while we're inside. We can talk to all the regulars, see if match the profile."

"These people need to get a life," Harley commented.

"Of course they do, they're undead," Del quipped, making Harley smirk and shake his head. "Let's just go in one car though. We don't want to look too conspicuous."

"Let me drive us there, Del," Harley said. "I've taken a great liking to driving lately."

"Yeah, I heard," he scoffed. "If you'd have been anybody else, you most definitely would have gotten yourself a ticket. Jones was just in too much shock, seeing you in whatever that get-up of yours was. Glad I didn't have to see it too. I mean, why would you want to get all vamped up in the first place?"

"Because it was fun," Harley chuckled. "It took him five minutes just to catch up to me."

"That may be, but we're on official police business in a police car right now, so you need to put yourself in check, boss."

"Yes sir, subordinate," Harley teased. "Just give me the keys."

"All right, but no speeding," he said as he handed them over. "And are you even going to ask me how to get there?"

"No, I already know where that place is," he said. "I considered it a waste of time."

"Hey, you're the one that's got the convoluted vampire theory, don't be raggin' on me for it," Del said. "You know the drill, get a profile and then follow the leads till they're all exhausted. Unless you want to change your opinion on this case?"

"No," Harley answered. "I stand by my original assessment. I'm just not so sure we're dealing with a pretender anymore."

"What are you talking about, Harley?" Del asked with a confused scowl. "Of course any vampire would have to be a pretender."

"Don't be so sure, my friend," Harley said. "After the week I've had, you'd be changing your mind too."

"Harley, just what the hell have you been doing all week that would lead you to believe in the existence of vampires?" Del demanded with an exasperated tone.

"Uh, let's see, I met one vampire who took me to a bar, and later I went to that bar again and met another vampire who took me to a party, where I met the other vampire again and also met one that I highly suspect is the killer," he said, ticking off his fingers one at a time. "Oh yeah, and everyone else at the party were also vampires—"

"Have you been taking any hallucinogenic drugs lately?"

"We're here," Harley announced with a grimace. "Please save this conversation for a later time. I don't need a flock of wannabes trying to pump me for information instead of the other way around."

"Right, boss," Del agreed. But he still kept giving him funny looks all the way to the door.

The pair strode up to the bar in a businesslike manner that clearly advertised that they were cops of some kind. Many of the people who were in the bar began to leave, so that the place looked practically deserted in less than two minutes.

"What do you want?" the barkeeper asked. "You're scaring away the customers."

"We're looking for Erick Strumpkull," Del told him. "We wanted to ask him a few questions in association with a case we're on."

"Blaze is one of the people you just scared off," the man told him with a raised brow.

"Any idea where he was going?" Harley asked in a slightly menacing tone.

"How should I know?" he said. "Listen, I just work for the guy. I'm not into all his hokey psycho-babble voodoo shit. I don't ask and he doesn't tell."

"Voodoo?" Del repeated. "What do you mean, voodoo? I thought he was into vampires."

"Yeah, but not every vampire originated in Transylvania, dude," he explained. "Blaze says most vampires you'd find around here were made somewhere in America, and that he was made a vampire in New Orleans."

"Ah, so he's delusional on more than one account," Del scoffed. "Listen, we've only got a listing for this place on him. Would you happen to have his home address or a number we could call or anything like that?"

"Blaze doesn't have an actual place," the barkeeper said. "Last I heard, his pack was partying hardy in some old, abandoned warehouse down near the waterfront. They never sleep, just sit around drinking each other's blood and getting high. In fact, I think they're holding a rave tonight, but I don't know exactly where. Maybe one of the regulars could help you out."

After questioning the remaining patrons—all four of them—the detectives were able to find out the general location of the rave, but no other information was forthcoming. They gave each of them a card, and the instructions to call if they remembered anything else, and then left to head for the waterfront.

Chapter Twenty

"Harley, I'm telling you, if we're going to go crash a rave, we need to bring back-up," Del insisted once again as Harley turned onto the old trucking road that wound along the beaches and serviced all the shipping companies that blanketed the general area.

"This is your bright idea, Del," said Harley with one brow lifted in his direction. "But if you were to call this in, what would you call it? We don't have a warrant, and by the time we got one the party would have moved on to somewhere else. Besides, we're not here to bust up the party. We're just looking for someone we want to question. There's no law that says we can't inquire about a specific person who may or may not be present. But if you go bringing in reinforcements for this, we'd get sued before you could whistle Dixie."

"Do you think you're suddenly invincible just because you're the man in charge?" Del wanted to know. "Look what happened to Jefferson. Do you want that to happen to you, too?"

"Look, Del, I can't explain the whole thing to you, just believe me when I say that I'm not a target—at least not at this point," Harley said as he ran a hand through his hair. "If I tried to tell you everything that's happened lately, you'd probably have me committed."

"You and I need to talk," Del said. "Seriously. Because this whole idea is whack!"

"Don't you want to follow the lead?"

"You lead and I'll follow," Del said. "You're about to get me killed."

"Del, you really need to learn not to be so tense," Harley told him. "Did you know that if you cease to care and just accept reality for what it is, that you could do anything you set your mind to?"

Del cast him a disgusted look.

"Yeah, I know, it sounds like some sort of a greeting card, right?" Harley chuckled. "But I'm beginning to think it's not as strange as it sounds."

"Let's go, Trent, before you start quoting even more greeting cards."

The two of them walked as casually as possible into the mass of drunk and high people who were all dressed like vampires, but who for the most part probably were not. At least, Harley didn't recognize any of these people from either of the parties he'd gone to.

Before too long, a tall man with thick black hair strode up to them. "Who are you two?"

"Nobody in particular," Harley answered. "We're just here looking for someone."

"We don't need any cops around here," he growled at them, baring his 'fangs'.

Instinctively, Harley laughed and bared his teeth at the man as well. A strange, tingling sensation gave him pause, however, and then he glanced at Del.

"What the hell, Harley?" Del gasped. "Are those really fangs?"

Harley put his hand up to his mouth in astonishment and touched the two large, protruding teeth he found there. "Yeah, I guess they are. Am I supposed to get fangs before the final bite?"

"Final bite?" the man repeated, so pale he almost looked completely white. "What the hell, are you one of the real ones? I've heard of you guys, but I didn't ever see one of you. Oh man, can you turn me, please? I'd give you anything you want."

"I'm no vampire," Harley said. "At least, I don't think I am. I don't remember her biting me a third time."

"What the hell are you talking about, partner?" Del demanded hotly. "Have you been running around with a pack of bloodsuckers all week?"

"I tried to tell you that earlier," Harley defended himself. "I'm supposed to be deciding whether or not to be a vampire, not sprouting fangs."

"Listen guys, could you keep it down?" said the wannabe. "If everyone here knew about this, it could start a riot, and every single one of them would be after you to bite them. This is a really bloodthirsty crowd."

"Who are you, anyway?" Harley inquired.

"They call me Blaze," he answered.

"Erick Strumpkull?" said Del. "You're just the man we're looking for."

"I am?" he asked. "What do you want me for? I haven't done anything."

"Other than host an illegal party ripe with all kinds of illegal drugs, hookers and biohazardous wastes being improperly disposed of," Harley added with a smirk.

"Um, what did you guys say you wanted, again?" he asked nervously.

"We're working on the Slayer case," Del told him. "We'd like to ask you a few questions pertaining to it."

"Oh no, man, you ain't pinnin' that shit on me," he said, his voice rising in anger now. "That guy is crazy, whoever he is. I heard about it on the news. He's been ripping people apart for years now, and you're no closer to finding him."

"Actually, Strumpkull, that's where you come in," Harley told him.

"How do you mean?" he wanted to know.

"I think you might be able to draw the killer out, so to speak."

"What did you have in mind?" he asked suspiciously.

"We leak it to the news you've been brought in for questioning as a possible suspect in the case," Harley explained. "If I'm right about him, this guy is going to be really upset that someone else is stealing his limelight. He'll try to discredit you, and if we're lucky when you are set free he'll try to follow you as well."

"What the hell, are you trying to use me like a chunk of meat on a fishing lure over top a bowl full of piranha?" he demanded. "You're trying to get me killed."

"Join the crowd," Del commented.

"Come on, Strumpkull, you're coming with us," Harley insisted.

"Okay, so whose going to alert the press?" Del wanted to know.

"I'll do it myself," Harley told them. "It's part of my job description."

Chapter Twenty-One

"Detective Trent, can you tell us anything about the man you currently have in custody? Is he a suspect in this case?" asked a female reporter who was up near the front of the huge crowd. Cameras flashed, and several video cameras took live action shots as well.

Harley stood up on a podium with about twenty microphones in his face. He held up his hands to silence the fifty other voices before he spoke.

"Okay, people, hold it down," he said, and the crowd grew a bit less noisy. "All I can tell you is that we are holding a man as a person of interest in the Slayer case. Whether we have our suspect or not has not been determined.

I'm sure you all understand that I cannot divulge a great deal about the man or his status at this time."

The babble of a hundred voices started in again, more insistent than before.

"Now, now, that's all I have to say on the matter," he insisted. "Thank you for your time, this press release is finished."

A whole bunch of the reporters tried to chase Harley inside as he walked resolutely away from them. It took several police officers to hold them back. Harley exchanged a glance with Del as he stepped inside, and the man fell into step with him.

"Do you really think this is going to work?" he inquired once they were out of earshot.

"I sure as hell hope so," Harley commented. "We can only keep Strumpkull here another thirty hours."

"That's true, but what have you learned from him in the meantime?"

"Well, you know how the bartender had said Strumpkull was using voodoo?" said Harley. "I asked him about it, and he said he didn't have any idea what the man was talking about. But I also managed to get his parent's address from the national directory database, and it appears that they do, in fact, live in New Orleans, and they run a little shop there called 'Magical Missives', I guess it's some kind of new age store. Anyway, I spoke to the mother, and she says that her son has been practicing magic most of his life. Now, what I don't get is, why wouldn't Strumpkull want us to know that?"

"A lot of magic practitioners are ridiculed these days," Del pointed out. "Some of them are treated to even more cruelty than just words. You do know, don't you, that it hasn't been all that long since the Salem witch trials, historically speaking. He could just be trying to save his skin."

"I've actually got a great deal of curiosity about magic myself," Harley admitted. "I've even studied quite a few books about it. But I just can't seem to shake the feeling that Strumpkull knows something about the vampires that he's not saying. I happen to know they keep humans to supply them with blood. How did she put it? like cows, I think that's what she said."

"'She' who, Trent?"

"Oh, never mind that," he hedged, realizing he'd been thinking out loud. "The point is, I'm wondering if Strumpkull and his cronies might be— well, blood donors, I guess you'd call them."

"Look, Harley, if I hadn't seen you sprout fangs with my own two eyes,

I'd be calling you a total lunatic right now," said Del as he crossed his arms and looked him over. "But it seems to me your neck deep in some serious shit, and I want to help. Isn't there anything I can do?"

"You can come with me to the castle," Harley suggested. "See it all for yourself, so to speak."

"Do I look like an idiot to you?" Del asked. "I'm not going near no damned castle full of bloodsuckers and becoming their next tasty treat, so you can forget it. And for that matter, you should probably steer clear of the place yourself."

"I don't think I can do that anymore, Del," Harley admitted. "I think it's already too late for me. I don't think you can just go back to being a regular guy again once you've started sprouting teeth and getting superhuman reflexes and all that. I mean, how would you?"

"Do I look like the answer man to you?" Del scoffed. "Hell, for all I know you're already a vampire and you just haven't figured it out yet."

"No, I'm neither one thing nor the other right now," Harley told him. "I can feel it in every cell, that I'm just not quite there yet. It's sort of building up in me, like a slow-moving virus. All I need is the final bite."

"Final bite?" Del repeated. "Are you listening to yourself, talking about needing the final bite? So what, you mean you've already been bitten and you didn't turn, so you're going to go get another bite to finish the job? What the hell is wrong with you? Do you want to become a vampire?"

"I—I don't know, Del, I just know that all my life I've known something was different about me, and now that I've met the woman of my dreams, I see things a whole lot clearer," he tried to explain. "Have I ever told you about my nightmares?"

"Yeah, a little," he answered.

"There is a woman in them—Vivianne," he said. "She was my wife, in another lifetime. In a lifetime during which I was a vampire."

"No," Del said hotly. "That's just a dream."

"It's no dream, Del," he insisted. "I've found Vivianne, and she's asked me to rejoin her. I don't know why I've been hesitant to do it anymore. It makes sense to me now, like I should have known it all along. I don't belong to this world; I have a much greater purpose. I have realized that if I turn, I could still help. I could right so many wrongs—I really could turn this city around. Can you imagine it, Del? I'd be a sort of superhero, maybe. It's what I've always wanted."

"You can't be serious," said Del as bile rose up into his mouth. "You would be feeding off people if you turned. Killing people—"

"No, they don't have to be killed, remember? They give their blood willingly in exchange for protection. They do things in the light of day so the vampires don't have to," Harley said. "It's a symbiotic relationship. I can see that now."

"No, Harley, whatever they've done to you is messin' with your mind," Del insisted. "They are brainwashing you, making you believe what they do is just, but in truth it's just plain sick. I can't believe you'd ever think that way!"

Del grabbed Harley by both shoulders and gave him a shake, but found he could not even budge him.

Harley gazed at him as though he were a mere fly buzzing about his head.

"Let go of me, Del," he ordered sharply, and Del dropped his hands, frozen with fear over the sound of his friend's voice.

"You're one of them already," he whispered as he stared at him.

Harley just laughed.

"I—I promise to keep this just between us, Harley," he said then, his body beginning to quake with fear. "You can trust me. You always have."

"I'm not going to hurt you, Del," Harley said with a laugh. "I just want you to come with me, to see for yourself. Maybe it's a life that you'd like, too."

"No, Harley," Del said. "I want to grow old. I want to die with grandkids and great-grandkids under my belt. I don't want to drink blood—not ever."

"I need to go," Harley told him. "I need to find Anne, tell her my decision is made."

"Don't do it, Harley," Del pleaded with him.

"I can trust you?" he asked again. "You'll keep your word?"

"I won't say anything, Harley," he answered. "I promise."

Chapter Twenty-Two

Harley went to the morgue to look for Anne, but the receptionist told him she wasn't there. Upset and uncertain, he decided to visit Demetrius even though it was not yet dark outside. The gear shift felt good in his hand as he sped through the streets like a bolt of lightning that had been set free to do as it pleased.

His whole body felt alive with need. Not just a need for Anne, but the need to be turned, for good or ill, rather than remain in this incessant state of limbo. He could almost remember what it had felt like, being a vampire, from the way he'd felt in his dreams.

He remembered the raw power, the heightened understanding and awareness of everything around him, and the rightness of the strong surviving by making use of the weak.

Demetrius was not in the Great Hall, not that Harley had expected him to be, but Anne was. She seemed to know somehow that he would be there. Knew, too, that he was searching for her. He understood this on some unseen, unspoken level deep within himself—they were linked in that way because she'd made him what he was.

"Anne, I—" he began.

"Hush," she said as she came over to him and wrapped him in her arms. "I know why you are here, Harley, but I want to make sure you know the whole story first. Come with me."

Wordlessly, Harley followed Anne up the newel staircase and down the long corridor to the room at the very end. She opened the door and held it for him, and followed in behind him, then shut the door tight and bolted it.

Harley's brow furrowed at this unusual extra step. Hadn't she said nobody would disturb them here? But that was on the night of the party. Perhaps things were different during the day. In any case, there were much more important issues to be dealt with first.

It was obvious by the sultry look in her eyes which order of business she thought took precedence. She was wearing a loose shift which tied between her breasts.

Now her hand came up to pull at the strings, her eyes never leaving his face as he glanced down at her heaving bosom. Her breaths were ragged, fierce even, and as soon as the clothing slid down her body and hit the floor she was on him, kissing him feverishly.

"Do you have any idea how much I want you, woman?" Harley asked her between the kisses. "I want you with all my soul."

"I want you, too, my beloved," she whispered. "Now and forever."

They fell together on the bed in a tangle of arms and legs, touching everywhere, and tasting as well. Harley managed to wrest free of her embrace enough to bend and take a pert nipple into his mouth. Anne groaned as he began to nip at it playfully.

"Harley, I want you inside me," she pleaded.

Never one to leave a lady in distress, Harley moved over her and plunged right in. Her gasp of pleasure was quickly followed by the walls of her vagina squeezing tighter as she came. The whole time he moved in her, the tightness remained, and she couldn't seem to hold back her cries of ecstasy as a result.

"Come in me, my love!" she finally gasped, and he complied rather quickly, her insatiable plea being the catalyst for his undoing. When they were done, they both lay there, completely spent.

After a while, Anne rolled onto her side to face him. Harley could tell by the look on her face that the next order of business was about to be discussed. He rolled on his side, too.

"Harley, I know how important your job is to you, and there's something I need to say," she told him. "Would you please listen to the whole story before you respond?"

"Of course," he agreed as he ran a hand down her arms in a slow, languid caress.

"I haven't told you everything there is to know about the past—yours, or mine," she said, then took a deep, shaky breath.

"Go on," Harley encouraged her.

"You know that I'm a vampire, but I don't believe you know exactly what that means," she said. "The vampires were spawned from the joining of Adam with Lilith. Unlike the demons, who were her first children, we are a blending of humans with the dark forces over which Adam's first wife held power.

"When our mother saw what she had created, she sent the vampires out into the world to feed upon the children of Eve, and at that time a sort of dark magic was born, enabling the vampires to live beyond the mere timeframe involved in a human's life. Every vampire's soul is immortal, even if their body dies. The body I reside in now is over nine hundred years old."

"You sure don't look it," Harley said.

Anne smiled wanly, and continued. "When you were made into a vampire, it was a use of that dark magic, and that made your soul immortal as a result. The same can be said of the vampire who eventually killed you. That vampire was the same one who had made you."

"You mean you didn't make me before?" he inquired.

"No, Harley, I was the one who created your maker, and so you became my responsibility when he—well, when he went feral, I guess you'd say," she said. "I did not sense the dissatisfaction within him until it was too late. He was cruel and selfish, and unworthy of the gift I had given him. You and I decided that he must be ended."

"You mean when I went to slay him, but he slayed me instead?"

"Yes, that was the day you tried," she said. "But you see, there is a part of that story that only your vampire self knows. You were able to obtain a magic spell that would entrap the soul of our nemesis from reincarnating yet again. You didn't take the time to reveal it to me, so I have never been able to take up where you left off."

"So, you're saying that if I become a vampire, I'd have the knowledge I gathered in the past so we could stop this monster for good?"

"Yes," she answered slowly. "But I don't want you to become a vampire just to solve the case. We're talking about a really, really long time here."

"I can imagine," he said, shaking his head. "Anne, when I came here I already had my decision made. I want to be with you, whatever it takes."

"No, I want you to wait," she said. "If only for a day. I know that you and Del are trying to lure out the killer with the suspect you brought in—I could sense this truth in you. Go back to work, stake him out as planned. I do not know which vampire is the feral one as yet, and your plan may flush him out. Once we know who we are dealing with, you can vamp out all you want."

"Why can't I solve the case as a vampire?" he asked.

"He would know you were after him."

"He already knows that," Harley said. "Why else would he be haunting my dreams?"

"Your life force is very strong," she told him. "More than one vampire would love to sink their teeth into you.

But you must let me be the only one. Understood?"

"Yes."

"Good," she said. "Think of me when you are ready. I will come to you then."

And with that, Anne became a silvery-colored bat and flew out the open window, leaving Harley all alone.

Chapter Twenty-Three

"Damn it, Harley, now look what you did," Del grumbled over the cell phone a few hours later. Harley had gone home for a bit to take a nap, and had been ignoring the house phone when the phone he'd forgotten to remove from his pocket disturbed his slumber as well.

"What do you mean?" he asked groggily.

"Aren't you watching the news?" he barked into the phone, prompting Harley to reach for the remote and start searching, bleary-eyed, for the right button to turn on the television.

"No," he finally said in defeat. "There's been another killing, much more brutal than the last," Del announced in disgusted tones. "We'd better get over to the station and get Strumpkull out of there. For all we know, that psycho will try to break in and get rid of him next."

"He'd be a fool if he tried," Harley pointed out. "The camera would catch him in the act."

"I thought vampires didn't show up in mirrors or on film," Del reminded him.

"Oh, I forgot about that," he answered, wondering if he'd be able to see himself in a mirror if he let Anne bite him again.

He padded into his bathroom and turned on the light. Well, at least he could still see himself at the moment. Would not being able to see himself make a difference to his decision? No, not really.

"Are you still there, Detective Trent?" Del demanded.

"I'm here," he answered as he began to brush his teeth. "Meet me at the station as soon as possible. And get Strumpkull out of that cell."

"Yes sir, boss man," Del agreed, and hung up on his end.

Harley pushed the end button, and stuffed his cell phone back into his pocket. After running a brush through his hair he exited the bathroom, stopped long enough to grab his coat, and headed out the door.

Demetrius was just exiting the elevator.

"What are you doing here?" Harley asked, not bothering to stop walking. When he passed the vampire, Demetrius simply turned and followed him.

"Just thought I'd come see how you're feeling," he said.

"What do you mean?" Harley asked.

"I thought you saw Anne today?" he answered as the elevator began its descent. "Didn't she bite you?"

"Not yet," he said. "She wanted to make sure I was—functional for the evening."

"You mean after all this time, when she's ready and you're ready, she decides not to bite you?" he said, clearly surprised. "Will wonders never cease."

"Not to be rude or anything, but I have got to get to work right now," Harley told him as the elevator came to a stop and the doors opened.

"Harley, wait," Demetrius said. "It won't be safe there right now."

"What are you talking about?"

"There's something I need to tell you," he admitted.

"I'm all ears," Harley said, though he was irritated by the interruption.

"It's—" he started, then swallowed hard before trying again. "It's about the Slayer."

"Go on," Harley answered, much more interested now.

"He's a friend of mine, I guess you'd say," he answered. "For the past thousand years or so, the soul within him has been running amuck, killing wherever and whenever it can. His is not a true vampire's soul, which can never die, but somehow, this soul has managed to find the way back time and again, always with disastrous results."

"And you know who the soul is now, what body it lives in?" Harley prompted.

"I do," he whispered. "Fool that I am, I'm the one who turned him again. He swore to me that this time things would be different. That this time, he would not release his rage upon the masses, but it seems he could not keep his word yet again."

"Why are you telling me this now?" Harley wanted to know.

"You are his eternal rival," Demetrius explained. "Ever since he turned you and then you rejected him in favor of Vivianne, he has vowed to end you once and for all. But Harley, you cannot possibly defeat him unless you are fully turned. You must return to Anne, for your own sake. Only your past memories contain the secret that will put a stop to his actions once and for all."

"Why would you wish to help me?" Harley asked him suspiciously.

"You said he was your friend, yet now you wish to betray him?"

"He is more than a friend to me, Harley," Demetrius explained. "We are lovers. We have been the whole time. But I have seen how wrong I've been, to set something so fierce and uncaring loose on the world. A vampire who does not honor our code, no matter who he is, must not be allowed to exist. I do not have the strength to do it myself, for my love is too great to overcome. But you—you, in a fully turned form—could end this vicious cycle once and for all."

"Where is Anne now?" Harley wanted to know.

"I don't know," he said. "I fear she may have gone to confront a few demons from her own past as well. She, too, was once under this soul's spell, until she met you. He has always preferred to surround himself with a variety of partners—another thing about him that wounds my heart. I fear I must leave you now, for I have much to do. But heed my words, Detective. Do not take him on before you are ready, or he will kill you once again."

In the blink of an eye, Demetrius was no longer beside him, and somehow Harley discovered he had walked all the way to his car without even being aware of their movement.

Shaking his head, he got in and turned the key. After taking a deep, shaky breath, he went back to the station as quickly as he could.

As he stepped inside, he could immediately tell that something was wrong. Usually in the middle of the night he had to buzz himself in, but as he pushed experimentally on the door it gave way freely, and he realized the lock was broken. Wary now, he squared his shoulders and stepped inside.

He walked briskly past the abandoned entry and on into the suite of offices beyond it. The building was almost completely vacant. Then he entered his own office and saw Del and Strumpkull sitting there, both unmoving as they stared with unseeing eyes.

Harley checked each man and found a pulse, then tried to shake Del awake. Beneath his feet, he noticed what looked like fog beginning to creep up around his ankles.

"What the hell?" he gasped, and began turning in circles as he always did in his dreams. It was at this point he began to wonder if this was really happening, or if it was a dream.

"Hello, Detective Trent," said a disembodied voice. "How have you been? You and I have missed our nightly battle over the last week, haven't we? Shall we dance again?"

"Where the hell are you, you sick bastard?"

"I am nowhere, Harley," he said, then laughed at his own joke. "I am invisible. At least, I am whenever I want to be."

"What have you done to these two?"

"They've been bitten, nothing more," he said dismissively. "And, oh yes, I remember now. I bit each of them three times already, so when they wake, they're going to belong to me. They're going to do whatever I want them to do. What do you suppose that might be?"

In a flash, Harley turned and headed for the exit, but doors started to slam all around, penning him inside. Desperate now, he returned to his office, watching the bodies with one eye as he looked at the window with the other.

"Stop him!" the voice shouted, and Strumpkull suddenly stood up and headed his way. Del stirred, but did not get up as well.

"I must thank you, Detective," Strumpkull said. "Thanks to you, I've been granted my fondest wish. And it looks like my first meal is going to be you. How poetic."

"Go to hell, Strumpkull!" Harley shouted.

"How original," he scoffed. "You can do better than that, can't you?"

Harley ran right through the window, glass shattering all around, and landed on his feet just outside, breaking into a dead run. Damn that freak to hell, he'd just taken Del away from him. Now, he was definitely going to pay.

Chapter Twenty-Four

Once he'd left the other vampires behind, Harley stopped to assess the damage he'd obviously done to his side. He was losing way too much blood. He needed to find Anne, and he needed to find her fast.

He hoped against hope that she would be at the morgue as he limped his way there and practically fell down the stairs. The receptionist took one look at him and sprang from her chair, helping him to sit down on the sofa and giving him a cloth to hold to the bleeding wound.

"Why didn't you go to the hospital, Detective?" she wanted to know.

"I don't want to be found," he said on a gasp. "Why are you still here, anyway? Isn't it the middle of the night?"

"They're making me work a double shift," she explained. "It's not like I have a life to worry about anyway. Just the same old, same old."

"Oh, so you get a lot of guys rushing in here bleeding to death?" he inquired with a chuckle that made his side hurt even more.

"I'll call Anne for you, sir," she said. "I know that's why you're here."

"Thank you," he answered, and leaned back to rest a bit.

A commotion in the hall upstairs had him sitting up again rather quickly.

"I know you're down there, Harley," Del shouted. "I just followed the blood trail."

"Damn it!" Harley hissed. "I need to hide."

"It's too late to hide, Harley," said Del as he came into the room. "You never should have come in here. This is all your fault I'm like this. I told you I didn't want to be a vampire, but oh, no, you had to go and provoke him. Now I have to destroy my best friend, and all because he couldn't keep his damned dick in his pants."

"I love her, Del," Harley told him as he scooted toward the other exit along the wall. "Why don't you be a pal, and pretend you didn't find me?"

"I have to obey my master," Del said with a disgusted scowl. "Whether I want to or not."

"That's not true," he said. "I escaped him before, didn't I?"

"And got yourself killed into the bargain," Del scoffed. "Yeah, I know the whole story—
he implanted it in my head, though he's got it twisted around to make him come

out smelling like a rose. So, you're trying to steal his girl, right?"

"Wrong," Harley growled.

"Vivianne was mine— Anne is mine now. He can go back to his male lover, and leave the two of us alone."

"Funny how he left that part out, isn't it?" Del scoffed. "Hey Harley, want to see a trick?"

"No," he answered as he reached the other door. Of course, Strumpkull was outside of it, standing guard.

"Here it goes," said Del, and fangs sprouted in his mouth as his face contorted into a grotesque version of its former shape.

"That's just nasty, Del," he informed him. "No wonder you don't want to be able to see yourself in a mirror. By the way, did you test out your theory? Can you be seen in a mirror or on a camera?"

"Yes, unless you know how to use an invisibility shield."

"Too bad for you, then, Del," he said. "There are cameras all over this place, as well as in the station. Everyone will know exactly what happened."

"I'll be sure to get rid of the evidence," Del told him, his large teeth making him lisp a little since he wasn't used to them.

"You sound funny," Harley commented, trying to make his friend laugh, to distract him.

"I'm going to miss your sense of humor, Harley," said Del with a shake of his head. "Most people didn't really get you, but me, I always understood. And now I understand even more than ever. How could you stand to be human all these years once you'd felt like this?"

"Because I didn't remember," Harley said. "I never could have stood it if I had."

"Hey, get away from me!" Strumpkull shouted from outside. Del and Harley turned in time to see a winged creature swoop down and carry him away. They both moved to the door, trying to see what was happening.

"Who—or what—the hell is that?" Del asked, his fangs no longer out.

"It's Anne," Harley said with extreme confidence. "If you don't take our side, I'm sure you're going to be next."

"There's nothing to stop me from killing you before she comes in," Del pointed out.

"If you really wanted to kill me, I'd already be dead," Harley countered in a reasonable tone.

"No, I just wasn't ready to do it—yet. My master would kill me for it if I didn't follow his orders," he answered, cringing at the thought.

"So what?" Harley pointed out. "I thought you didn't want to be a bloodsucker anyway."

"You always did know how to make me laugh," Del said again, and Harley looked over at him uncertainly. Then he saw that Del was holding a large wooden stake in his hand. The pointed end was not directed at Harley, but at himself.

"What are you doing?" Harley shouted, moving to take the stick from his hands. But Del drove it into his chest before he could stop him.

"Maybe we'll meet again sometime," he whispered as he fell to the floor.

"Why did he do that?" asked the receptionist from her desk. Then she snapped her gum and went right back to doing her nails again.

"Um, you really do get this kind of thing in here every night, don't you?" Harley asked as he took in her completely unruffled demeanor.

"Yeah," she said. "It kind of goes with the territory."

"Harley?" Anne called as she hurried in the door. He wanted to turn and nonchalantly greet her, but he was too dizzy from the blood loss, and fell down at her feet instead.

She scooped him up and cradled him in her arms as she transformed again and flew the two of them away.

"Where are we going, my love?" Harley whispered.

"Someplace safe," she said. "Somewhere we can be alone."

"You know there's only one way to save me now, don't you, Anne?"

Harley asked her, and felt the tension in her body seeping slowly away.

"We will take care of it, just as soon as we get there," she answered. "Now be quiet, and save your strength. Everything will be all right soon."

Chapter Twenty-Five

Harley wasn't certain when he'd passed into unconsciousness as Anne carried him in her arms. Her leathery wings beat at a steady tempo, lulling him into a stupor aided by his loss of blood. They could have been flying for minutes, or hours, for all he could tell.

Everything was hazy as he lie wherever it was she'd brought him, and he vaguely recalled that she had bitten him one last time. Or was that just a dream? The fine line that had been drawn for some time between the two worlds seemed to fade away.

A constant fog plagued him, and visions accosted his eyes. Visions of other times, other places, in a long, unending stream, taking him further and further into the past.

Then, quite suddenly, the haze was gone.

"Open your eyes, Harley," Anne continued to plead, and this time he heeded the words.

"Where am I?" he rasped through a swollen throat. He did not want to know what would have been the cause.

"Safe," she answered. "At least, safe for the moment."

"What do you mean?" he whispered as he turned his head to look around. They appeared to be in some sort of well-lit cave. The light hurt his eyes, and he threw up a hand to shield them as he groaned with pain.

"Just wait a few moments, Harley," she told him. "Your eyes must become accustomed to the Sight, now that your transformation is complete."

"So you did bite me, then?" he clarified. "It wasn't just a dream?"

"If I hadn't, you would not be here to ask," she said, slightly defensive.

"No, Anne, don't feel ashamed," he said softly, reaching for her hand and grasping it in his. "You know that I wanted this. Wanted to be with you always."

"And wanted to regain your memories, so you could solve your case," she said softly.

"I guarantee you that was only a very small part of the decision," he told her, drawing her down on top of him so he could hold her in his arms. "You have haunted my dreams as far back as I can remember—not just the dreams of Harley Trent, but every one of the other five beings that I was before him. You are my destiny, Anne. Our fire is undying."

"I love you, Harley," she whispered against his lips before she claimed them for her own. She kissed him so thoroughly he wasn't even able to say the words back for several minutes.

"My love, there is little time," he told her. "I must try to remember how to stop the Slayer, and that memory has not yet come. What can I do to revive it?"

"I fear there is only one way," she answered. "You must feed."

"Feed?" he repeated in annoyance. "But how will I do that without help from someone who may very well be the suspect?"

"Demetrius will help us," she answered. "He is one of the old ones, the true vampires. It is not in his nature to allow a fledgling to hunger."

"Anne, wait," he said urgently. "Demetrius told me that the Slayer is his lover. He must know who he is. Is there no way we can convince him to reveal the name of the perpetrator?"

"Demetrius told you that?" she gasped.

"He told me that we must destroy the killer once and for all," Harley said. "But I can't remember how."

"Magic," she answered. "Black magic at its blackest. We must find the Necromancer of Fagon—it was he who taught you once before, and lost that body in the teaching. We'll have to determine who he is now, I'm afraid."

"And how do we find him?"

"There is only one way," she said. "We must go to Fagon itself. Surely his soul has not abandoned the city of its birth."

"Fagon? Are you talking about the mythical place beyond the veil of faerie?" Harley asked. "I've only heard of it within my dreams."

"You know of it only because you have been there yourself," she said. "Even I have seen it only once, many centuries ago. It is a place of great power—
a power that has been lost to the modern world. It now exists only for those who still believe."

"How do we get there?" Harley asked as he tried to sit up and found that he could not.

"We must deal with first things first," she reminded him. "We are deep within the earth at the moment, my dear. I will have to travel to Demetrius in a dream if I wish to contact him from this place. Rest now, my love, for I too must sleep."

Harley insisted. "I'm worried about telling Demetrius where we are, Anne. What if he tells the Slayer of our whereabouts? I am in no condition to fight anyone yet."

"Harley, I know that Demetrius will help," she insisted. "Why would he have come to you and told you of his lover if he did not intend to take your side? A vampire does not offer information lightly, and they are even less likely to offer help they do not intend to give. You are worried over nothing, I can assure you."

"Anne, I must know something," Harley said as he grasped her hand again. "Who made you? Are you a daughter of Lilith and Adam, or were you born human?"

"I was made by my uncle," she explained. "I am the child of a vampire female and a human male. My mother's brother and she herself were children of Lilith. They had existed for thousands of years before my birth. My father was turned, of course, and helped in my upbringing."

"What year were you born?"

"1067 A.D.," she answered. "I was born just as England fell to the Conqueror."

"That's a long time," he commented. "And when was my soul first turned?"

"Not until 1284," she said. "Slayer was your maker."

"You mean to tell me I'm plotting to kill my own father, of sorts?" Harley chuckled wryly. That sounds like an appropriately evil thing for a creature of the night to do."

"Ha!" she snorted. "Don't let anyone down here hear you say such things. We don't need to make even more enemies than we have already."

"Others?" Harley asked. "There are others here? What others?"

"We are in an underground vampire sanctuary, of sorts," she answered. "But I must tell you, not everyone here is friendly to our cause. Some of them would kill us for even contemplating the idea of killing a soul. We must leave this place soon, and tell no one of that departure."

"Is there no way to simply imprison Slayer's soul instead?" Harley asked. "To compel it not to go feral again?"

"That has been tried already," she answered. "We're going to have to contact Demetrius. Lie quiet now, Harley. I must go to sleep, if I am to get you the help you need."

With a heavy sigh, Harley subsided. He was asleep even before Anne's thoughts had begun to drift, and she followed him to dreamland very soon afterward.

Chapter Twenty-Six

When Harley opened his eyes again, Anne was pacing back and forth nervously. He watched her for a time, enjoying the gentle sway of her hips, the smooth, delectable line of her body as she moved with catlike grace. After a moment, she glanced up as she sensed his scrutiny.

"He should be here soon," she told him as she ceased her movements.

"Don't stop on my account," he teased her.

"Men! Even when they are half dead they still think only of one thing," she said with a chuckle as she came to sit beside him.

"What do you mean, half dead?" he wanted to know. "This thing is completely awake."

"Is it?" she inquired, her eyes lighting up as she scrutinized his crotch with interest.

"Maybe you should see for yourself," he suggested.

"Demetrius will be here any minute," she reminded him with a chuckle.

"Oh, that's okay, he doesn't mind a good show," Harley teased her as he wiggled his hips.

"Maybe just a taste," Anne said wickedly as she brushed her cheek over the area in question. Her fingers slid tantalizingly up to grab the zipper, and then she slowly pulled it down. She undid the button at the top, and slid his underwear down, out of the way.

Harley groaned with pleasure as her sweet mouth encircled his rigid flesh. His hands slid down into her hair, playing with her curls.

"Just don't bite that thing," he reminded her, making Anne giggle. She ran her tongue all along him, from shaft to balls, and then playfully made her fangs appear, just enough to notice.

"Why not?" she purred.

"Anne, behave yourself or I'll have to give you a spanking," he said with a laugh. They both knew he could barely move, so who did he think he was fooling?

"Idle threats do not sway me," she told him, trying to keep her expression serious but failing miserably. "You're just going to have to do something to keep my mouth occupied if you want me to be good."

Harley used his hands, which were already nesting in her hair, to bring her face up to his and kiss her. Their tongues danced together as Anne's hand came up to cup his exposed balls.

"I wouldn't want these to get too cold," she said as she played with them.

"With you around, that would never happen," he told her, then experimentally made his own fangs come out as she'd done earlier, and nipped at her lips with them. She gasped at the sensation and did it back. Both of them laughed again.

"Are you two actually going to do something over there, or are we going to give the man what he really needs?" Demetrius asked with some amusement.

The amorous couple kissed once more before they broke apart. Harley put his pants back in order as he tried to sit up, but found he was too weak to do so and laid back again.

"Look at you, Harley, in such a sorry state," Demetrius said as he shook his head. "It's a good thing I'm the only one who knows where you are, or you'd be a sitting duck in this deplorable condition."

"The bastard pulled a fast one," Harley said. "He won't find it so easy to do again, now that Anne has turned me."

"Drink this," said Demetrius as he held up a soft drink cup with a straw. Looking at it dubiously, Harley sipped the liquid inside down hungrily. As he drank, he could feel his strength returning, and growing, until it was ten times that of his human form, if not more.

"Anne tells me the two of you may need to travel outside the country," Demetrius said.

"Yes, to the city of Fagon, of all places," Harley answered as he wiped at his mouth and then sucked the fluid he'd removed off of his hand.

"Fagon is not as easy to find as you might think," Demetrius explained. "It's not so much a matter of finding its location, as it is finding a way past the guards. They've been instructed to kill anyone who makes the attempt to enter."

"Even someone who has been invited?" asked Harley curiously.

"Yes, everyone," he said. "That way, only those worthy of the place ever manage to get in. But, as you've been there before, it shouldn't be as difficult for you a second time around."

"Yeah, if I could just remember what exactly I did before that worked," Harley pointed out. "I thought I'd have all of my memories back by now, but nothing has changed."

"Let the blood get into your system," Demetrius suggested. "You'll feel better soon enough."

"I really must thank you for all your help," Harley said, shaking his hand.

"You're welcome," Demetrius said. "But I help you mostly because it is your task to complete, and yours alone. If you do not stop the Slayer, then no one will."

"I'll do my best," Harley answered.

"That's all any of us can do," he said as he turned to go.

"Now, the question is, do we want to travel to England above ground, or would it be safer to take the tunnels?" Anne asked.

"Although it may take you longer, I believe the tunnels will be safer," Demetrius cautioned, turned back to them again. "As long as you avoid the indigenous life forms who want to eat you."

"If we go through the tunnels, we'll probably have to eat the indigenous life forms ourselves if we hope to arrive intact."

"Yes, there is that possibility," he agreed. "But, I have brought you a large supply of blood just in case."

"Thanks, my friend," she told him. "We're both in your debt."

Demetrius laughed. "Very well then, I'm sure I'll think of a repayment ere you return."

"I'll bet you will," said Anne, and she held out her hand for Harley to take.

Together, the pair of them left Demetrius far behind as they headed deeper into the cave they were in. Harley didn't really like the thought of digging himself an even deeper hole, but he was willing to trust the judgment of the two more knowledgeable vampires. What they did now might just be the only way they would live to tell their tale.

Chapter Twenty-Seven

Harley was confused for a while as to how they had continuous light with no light source, until it dawned on him that there was no light source, but rather that his eyes were able to see in the dark as if there was one. He took a moment or two to consider how awesome that was before he dismissed the thought completely.

Anne still had ahold of his hand as they practically ran through the caves at a steady pace. He wondered why they hadn't turned into bats and flew but then they got into a space so tight it would have not allowed them to spread their wings, and he knew his answer.

He didn't exactly know why it was he did not wish to speak, he just felt compelled to keep silent. When he kicked a rock and it hit the wall of the cave with a thud, it echoed for several seconds, and Anne cast him a dubious look. He shrugged an apology and decided he'd best be more careful.

It seemed like hours passed as they continued to lope along through the underbelly of the Earth. Finally they stopped near an underground stream—more like a lake, really. Anne whispered in his ear, "Drink, Harley. There's too much sulfur in the water for a human, but we are able to tolerate it."

Harley nodded and leaned down to take some water into his mouth. He spit it out in disgust, making Anne laugh.

"I never said it tasted good," she mentioned in as soft a voice as possible. "Come, it is unwise to linger by the watering hole, even underground."

Seeing the sense in that statement, Harley nodded as he took her hand again. When she stopped suddenly after only a minute of walking, Harley froze as well. The sounds of nearby movement were unmistakable.

"Who—or what—is it?" he whispered.

Anne held a finger to her lips and went down a side cave they were conveniently near. Just inside the opening she hunkered down to watch, and Harley instinctively went to the other side of the entrance to do the same. His heart thudded louder than usual in his chest, and he could feel his fangs itching to come to the surface.

His eyes widened in surprise as about four demons walked by, laughing amongst themselves. Then he heard Anne's voice speaking inside his head:

"Children of Lilith. But we do not know if these are friend or foe. Some of the tribes hate the vampires, and some help them. We must wait until we are sure."

Harley cast her a confused glance. Sure of what? he thought, trying his best to send the thought her way. He half suspected it was his facial expression, rather than any successful sending, that caused her response.

"Sure which way the lava flows," she silently sent back.

Harley suppressed a chuckle at this. Of course it would not be 'which way the wind blows' in a place that had no wind. But he wondered if she ever used the more familiar connotation when she was not underground.

After a time, the demons returned from the watering hole, each one carrying a clay pot which Harley assumed they had filled. It wasn't until that moment he realized these were females.

They must be gathering water for their tribe to use—maybe even during an upcoming meal. He hadn't ever thought about what demons did for dinner before.

"Scurough!" one of them said, stopping just outside the opening. "We can smell you, lesser children. You may as well come out."

Anne cast a glance at Harley, and together the pair of them stepped out into the main cavern again. "We mean no disrespect to you, greater children," she said, bowing to the female who had spoken. "We are merely passing through. My fledgling has a great need to enter Fagon."

"A noble ambition," she said, and turned her eyes to Harley. "And an excellent choice. He is a fine specimen.

I would have turned him myself, if I were you."

Blushing, Harley said, "Thanks—I think?"

The females laughed, and Anne joined in.

"You must teach this one demon etiquette, my dear," she said with an indulgent smile. "In our world, fledgling, a male only addresses a female if he wishes to mate."

Harley's jaw dropped as he looked over to Anne for confirmation, and she chuckled again. "Don't worry, Harley, she is just trying to tease you. She knows you are my mate."

At the sound of those words, Harley could not help but swell with emotion. Yes, he was Anne's mate. He hadn't allowed himself to realize that fact yet, but it sat well with him now that the words were spoken.

"Always and forever," he said as he cast her an affectionate smile.

"This one loves you," said the demoness. "That is even better. We will escort you to our people for a time. The king would not wish you to pass through his lands without paying your proper respects."

"A wise observation," Anne agreed. "It has been so long since I've been down here, I no longer remember where my allies live and where the others lie in wait. I believe your king should have a map for me, is that not so?"

"He will most gladly furnish one, I'm sure," she agreed. "I am Ophala, and these are my sisters, Fojena, Elura, and Phasia. We are the water gatherers, as you may have guessed."

"I am Vivianne le Fade, and my fledgling's human name was Harley

Trent," said Anne with a smile. "He has yet to determine if there will be another."

"What's wrong with the one I have?" Harley wanted to know.

"Nothing, my dear," she said. "You may keep it as long as you are able."

"Come, let us depart ere someone from the other clan arrives," Ophala said uneasily. "They are no friends to the lesser children. I do not wish for them to start another war simply because of your presence."

Both Harley and Anne fell into step with them as the demons led the way to their home.

)0(

As the water gatherers approached the stone pillars that

marked the entrance to their city, young ones spotted their guests and began to flutter about excitedly. One intrepid youth fluttered right over to the group excitedly.

"Mother? Mother, who is this you've brought to the city?" she exclaimed as she circled Ophala's head three times and alit on her shoulder.

"Off, off, Oledana, you're getting too big to perch on me," Ophala complained. "It won't be much longer before you accompany me to fetch the water yourself."

"Oh, yes!" she exclaimed. "I can hardly wait!"

"We found these lesser children wandering through the main cavern, and thought they'd like to pay homage to the king," Ophala told her. "Now hush, child, or you'll wake the elders before it is time for the meal."

The young demoness cringed at this idea, and subsided rather quickly.

"What's the big deal with waking the elders?" Harley whispered to Anne.

"Have you ever seen a cranky elder, fledgling?" Ophala asked with a smirk. "It's not a pretty sight."

"I'll take your word for it," Harley said, cringing himself now. He seemed to have a very vague recollection of a huge demon unfurling its wings as it shouted out in rage, but he couldn't recall where or when he'd obtained such a memory. Then he realized that it wasn't his memory at all; it was coming from Anne. He smiled over at her and nodded, and she smiled in return.

They trudged along the narrow entrance for a few yards before it widened out into a vast cavern, larger than Harley ever dreamed possible. The expanse was littered with buildings of rock as far as the eye could see. Off in the distance stood a huge stone castle, obviously the home of the king, and their destination.

"It is easier to fly from here, if your fledgling has learned," Ophala told Anne.

"He hasn't tried as yet," she answered uncertainly.

"I'll give it a shot," Harley said. "Just tell me what to do."

"Think with your whole body that you wish to fly," Anne said. "If you want it badly enough, you will sprout wings."

Harley concentrated hard, and suddenly felt the wings sprout from his back. He grinned at the women triumphantly.

"That's good, fledgling," Ophala told him. "Now all you have to do is figure out how to use them. Good luck!"

And with that, she and the other demons flew off toward the castle, leaving Anne and Harley behind.

"Come on, then," Anne said. "Don't let her intimidate you. You can do it."

Harley tentatively flapped until his feet left the ground, then with one strong thrust he was in the air, flying after the others. With a delighted laugh, Anne caught up with him.

"Just remember, Harley, it's one thing to fly in a straight path," she said. "You will still need to learn how to steer."

"This is great!" he shouted joyfully. "I've always wanted to be able to fly!"

"Well how about flying toward the castle instead of away from it?" Anne asked with some amusement.

Harley had been looking at her and angled his wings differently as he did so, and now he noticed he'd drifted far to the left.

"Oops," he answered, and righted himself. They did not speak again until they landed in the courtyard, where the demons were waiting for them.

"So, I see you've made it in one piece," Ophala teased Harley. "But now you're about to enter a building full to the brim with all manner of Lilith's children. It may be a huge culture shock to one such as you."

"I can manage," Harley answered bravely. "I mean, how bad can it be?"

Again with the laughter. It was starting to annoy him. But he'd show these women that he was man enough to get through this entire adventure unscathed. Then who would be laughing?

Chapter Twenty-Eight

In the Great hall—which was a much greater size than he'd expected—were creatures of all shapes and sizes. Whoever the person was who supposedly had studied all about demonology and made a book showing what they looked like and such didn't even scratch the surface. And, contrary to popular belief, not everyone present was red and cloven-hooved either.

There seemed to be a large number of youngsters fluttering about, some of them serving the food. Harley could not identify the animal that had been roasted whole and set before the king, and he was rather put out that the king did not see them immediately upon their arrival. Apparently food was more important than business.

"Don't worry so much, fledgling, the king is most definitely aware of your presence," Ophala consoled him as he sat picking at the food on his plate. "You may as well fill your belly, for he won't see you until his own is full, and he is quite a bit hungrier than you."

Harley smirked at this pronouncement, for the king was at least three times his size, and even wider than he'd be at that size while he was at it. There could be no denying his appetite, for he ate four of the strange looking animals all to himself along with generous helpings of the roots and other plants on the menu.

Rolling his eyes at the outspoken female, Harley ate as much food as possible in the remaining time just to keep her quiet. He imagined that if vampires suffered headaches, he'd probably have one at the moment.

For that matter, how would he know whether or not vampires suffered headaches? Had anyone non-vampirical asked a vampire if they suffered from headaches? One could get a headache just from wondering that, as well.

Anne grasped Harley's shoulder and gave it a squeeze. "Stop trying to overanalyze everything, Harley. You're not conducting an investigation here." Harley cast her a smirk. She was right on the money with that one. If there was one thing about himself that he knew for a fact could never change, it was his analytical nature. But, truth be told, he didn't want to change it anyway. It had gotten him out of more scrapes than he cared to remember.

"You're right, Anne," he finally said when she kept watching him. "I guess I am thinking too much. But I'm new to this vampire thing, you know. There's so much I don't know yet."

"You know, my love, you've just forgotten," she said. "Give it a few days, and all those answers will just pop right in your head like old friends. You just wait and see if they don't."

"The king will see you now," Ophala told them.

Harley stood and followed behind the guard who had been sent to fetch them, and Ophala gave Harley an encouraging wave as he glanced back and noticed she was not going to accompany them. Anne took his hand in hers and gave it a squeeze.

"Just be polite, Harley," Anne told him. "He's not likely to bite—I hope."

"What do you mean, you hope?" asked Harley, not liking the sound of that.

"Well, he might want to mark us as under his protection," she explained. "Usually that's done by him biting your right arm—kind of like a tattoo, only one that carries a distinct odor that all other creatures down here recognize. I'm actually hoping that he'll do this, truth be told. It may save us a few troubles along the way."

"If there's any biting to be done, I'd rather it be you who bites me," Harley whispered suggestively in her ear.

"Mm, maybe later," she answered.

Then they were standing before the king, so there was no more time for banter. Each of them bowed, and then the king waved them over to a couple of chairs that had been furnished for them.

"So, lesser children, what brings you to my kingdom?" the king asked in a great, booming voice that shook the stalactites above them. This did not bring Harley any comfort as he paused to see if any would break free.

Anne answered for them. "We are on a quest, Majesty," she said. "We wish to enter Fagon as soon as possible, as one of the lesser children has gone feral and my fledgling has been charged with ending his tyranny."

"I seem to recall a similar quest about a millennium ago," he said curiously. "I never met the vampires that time, though. Do you know of this?"

"Harley is a reincarnate," Anne told him. "We have not yet recovered his memories of old. Perhaps his ancestor may be who you are thinking of, but alas, the feral was not stopped at that time, and his body was destroyed in that attempt."

"Well, Master Harley, let us hope that you fare better on this attempt," the king said magnanimously. Then he grabbed up the right hand of each of them, and stuffed their arms into his mouth up to the shoulder, biting them.

When he spit the arms out again, he said, "You will go with my seal upon you, my friends. Though I do not know how much comfort this will bring once you reach the pits. Many evils have been gathering there as of late."

"We thank you, Your Majesty, for your generosity," Anne said, bowing her head. "Tell me, have you a current map of the Underdwell? It is many centuries since last I came below."

"I shall have my servants bring you the newest one we have," he offered. "But for now, it would be wise for you to rest for a time. You are welcome to stay in the city for a day or two, to get your bearings before you forge ahead."

"Thank you, sire," Anne said, bowing her head again.

"Yes, thank you," Harley added, bowing his head as well.

"He is a quick study," the king smiled. "With any luck, he will remember what he's about before you set out again. Now, I bid you good journey. May your dreams guide your path."

Both Harley and Anne bowed as they stood to follow the servant who now stood beside them. The stone building they were given was roomy, and the bed was quite cozy. They were given warmed ale to help them relax, and a fire had been lit in the hearth near the foot of the bed.

"This is going to put me to sleep," Harley complained. "I wasn't ready for that quite yet."

"What is it you're ready for, my love?" Anne asked with a smirk.

"You know very well," he teased her as he pulled her down into the pillows with him. "Demetrius may have interrupted us before, but I doubt we'll be disturbed this time."

"I don't think we will be," she agreed as her lips traced a path from his ear to his neck. Barely allowing her fangs out, she playfully nibbled along his jugular vein, then licked at it. He'd had no idea just how arousing that could be until right that moment. Pushing her into the pillows, he pounced on her throat and did it back.

"Oh! Bite it, Harley," she pleaded. "Claim me, my mate!"

Harley let his fangs sink into her neck, drawing just enough blood to smear it around a bit, covering her throat. Then he spent several minutes tasting and licking it off again. Anne was in a frenzy of need by the time he'd finished, and she tore off both of their clothes and cast them aside.

Harley laid her in the pillows again, and mounted her. As his hardened cock slid in, he realized that it felt bigger than he remembered. Hmm, vampire perks, he thought with a smile. Then he set to the task of making his lovely Anne scream his name incessantly over the next few hours.

Chapter Twenty-Nine

"So, do you remember anything?" Anne inquired when Harley opened his eyes. He had no idea how long he'd been sleeping, but it was long enough to begin craving blood again. She was quick to remedy this, however, by handing him a warmed drink. It needed salt, was his first thought. But beggars couldn't be choosers.

His wayward mind began to wonder how one would know which blood would be more salty if he had to select a victim, but he shook that thought away forcefully. He would not be choosing victims, only volunteers. "I can remember the most incredible session of lovemaking ever," he told her with a grin. "Are you ready for another go?"

Anne chuckled and slapped at his questing hands, but she didn't try overly hard to escape, either. They kissed hungrily, but then she remembered what they were supposed to be doing and put him resolutely away from her.

"The map is here," she said. "We need to plot the best path."

"I like this map better," Harley said, tracing a path from her breast to her mons. "Hmm, a secret cave. I'd like to explore that."

"You are completely and irrevocably horny," Anne accused him.

"Guilty," he acknowledged, drawing her back into his arms. He easily slid inside her, proving that she was just as willing as he. "Damn, you are so sweet," he told her then.

"Shut up and fuck me," she told him, covering his mouth with kisses until he had nothing left to say. Moving in her with a heady abandon, Harley savored her lips and tongue as he did so, tasting and tantalizing an orgasm right out of her. And when she'd begun, his hands snaked up to her hardened nipples just to add even more intensity. Anne writhed beneath him, her walls clenching so tight he could not help but follow her into the abyss.

"I lied," he told her as they lay together in the afterglow.

"Hm? What did you lie about?"

"About the best bout of lovemaking ever," he teased her. "I think we just topped it."

"I think you're right," she agreed. "Now we should probably have a look at this map—and don't try sexing me up on top of it, either. You might make it smear with your love juices."

"My love juices?" Harley chuckled.

"Yeah, you know, sweat, saliva and semen."

"You forgot one," he said with a grin.

"Did I?"

"Yes, what about your love juice? Women have some, too," he reminded her, and stuck in a finger to get some, then put it into her mouth. Anne giggled around his finger.

"What's so funny?" Harley wanted to know.

"It tastes like you."

"Just get the map, woman, before I decide to make you taste even more like me than you already do."

Laughing mischievously, Anne grabbed the rolled up animal hide and laid it out flat in the middle of the bed. She pointed out areas they ought to avoid, and then traced a path from where they were to where they wanted to go.

"That's at least a six day journey," she told him. "Depending upon how fast we move, and how easy it is to bypass these areas here. The life forms in these three areas are most definitely not friendly towards us."

"Why are the vampires called the lesser children?" Harley asked her.

"Lilith was a great and powerful demoness, but she lowered herself to mate with a human," Anne explained. "From the moment the progeny were born, the others she'd birthed of her own body were jealous and disgusted by them. Jealous because the new ones had two parents, but disgusted because that other parent had shunned us, so we must therefore be inferior. But even though all demons call us lesser, many of them consider us equals. It is only a select few among them who wish to see us completely destroyed. Those haters will not hesitate to kill, no questions asked. It is best to avoid them at all costs."

"Sounds like a lovely family tree you've got there," he teased her. "But me, I prefer loving over fighting."

Harley grabbed Anne around the waist and laid her on top of the map. She giggled the whole time as he began a slow exploration of her anatomy with his tongue, ending up between her legs. She laughed even harder when he said, "So that's what I taste like."

"Stop it!" she begged, but to no avail. However, she did stop laughing at that point, because what he was doing started to feel really good. Her giggles soon became groans, and then Harley mounted her right on top of the map, making her laugh a bit more.

"What's the matter?" he inquired innocently.

"I was just wondering if he's going to want this back," she commented wryly.

"Well, let's make sure we give it back to him well used, then," Harley chuckled.

"You're terrible," Anne told him. Then Harley made her come about four times before he finally let her go. After they lay there for a few minutes, she said, "Maybe not all that terrible."

Harley laughed, and so did Anne. They laughed themselves silly, and then Anne decided to roll up the map again.

"This has been fun, but we really must begin our journey anew," she told him. "Now at least we'll have an idea where to go—and where not to."

Chapter Thirty

After taking their leave of the king, Harley and Anne headed for the stone pillars that marked the edge of the city on the far side. As they walked swiftly, Anne became aware of young Oledana fluttering along behind them, using the buildings to hide herself.

"I think we have a companion," she told Harley. "I hope Oledana is not foolish enough to follow us outside the city walls."

"I'm sure she's just being curious," Harley said. He had also been aware of her presence for some time now.

"Oledana, I know you are following us," Anne called to her. "Come out, child."

"I'm not a child," she protested as she flew out from behind the nearest building. "My mother said I'm almost big enough to help gather water."

"Well, that is because the watering hole is only a short trek from the city. Where we are going, we will be many days journey from it," Anne said gently.

"I could be a big help," she insisted. "I know how to find water anywhere."

"You need to stay with your mother," Anne insisted. "Have you ever spent any time away from her, Oledana?"

"Well, no, but how hard can it be?"

"Harder than you might think, my dear," said Anne. "Now go on, perhaps you will see us again on the way back."

"Oh, all right," she grumbled, fluttering away with a dejected air.

Harley smiled. "You handled that well," he said. "I know exactly how she feels, though. I remember what it was like, feeling grown up but not quite there."

"Yes, so do I," said Anne. "But for me, that was a very long time ago."

The two continued on in companionable silence, and soon the city was far behind them. They were just coming upon a water source when they heard some rocks tumbling somewhere behind them.

"You don't think—" Harley began.

"Definitely," Anne answered, turning to go back to the source of the sound. Oledana looked up at her sheepishly and shrugged. "What do you think you're doing? We don't have time to take you back home."

"I was sort of counting on that," she admitted as she hung her head, though it was obvious that she didn't really feel sorry for what she'd done.

"Well, come on then," Anne said gruffly. "I hope you're able to keep up the pace, young one. We're trying to get through here quickly."

"I've come this far, haven't I?" she pointed out proudly.

"We've only been walking for a few hours," Anne reminded her. "We intend to keep up this pace for several days. And there's a lot of dangers out here I'll bet your mother never even told you about, for fear you'd never sleep again."

"It can't be that bad," she scoffed.

"We'll see about that," Anne said as she turned and headed back toward Harley. "If you're lucky, you won't have to find out."

Now Oledana's eyes were jewel-bright with excitement as she followed along behind the vampires. She was actually on an adventure!

Harley said, "Are you any good at tracking anything besides water? I really liked those berry-flavored roots we had at dinner yesterday."

"What is yesterday?" she asked, crinkling her nose at him.

"I suppose you don't know what day and night are, do you?" he answered. "Way up above the ground, where humans dwell, we have a sky. In the sky are two different light sources. One is the sun, and one is the moon and stars. In the day, the sun makes more light than you have ever seen, and if you looked right at it, your eyes would get burned. Sort of like looking into fire. But at night, the moon shines. It is a soft, wonderful light that makes everything dance with shadows, especially when it's full."

"I wish I could see the sun and the moon," Oledana told him. "Someday I will find my way up to the outer world, and see all the wonderful sights."

"It would be far too dangerous for you, my dear," he told her. "The children of Lilith are mostly unwelcome there. Most humans don't even believe you exist at all, or that if you do, you must be evil simply because that is what they've been told."

"Some of the old ones enjoy being evil sometimes," she conceded. "But that's mostly because they have nothing better to do."

"So demons come up and terrorize humans because they're

bored?" Harley inquired with a chuckle. "I always kind of thought so."

"Oh yes, and the males sometimes go there as a maturity rite," she added. "Once they've gone there, even if just for a few minutes, they get to brag about it forever, just like my brother. He's always bragging about his adventures when he comes home."

"Yes, that's the only trouble with adventures," Harley said. "While we're on them, we don't get to be at home, and our loved ones tend to miss us until we return."

Oledana sighed. "I know what you are trying to say," she said. "My mother will be very worried about me. But friend Harley, did you never wish to strike out on your own, and prove to yourself that you were more than just a youngling? When I return to my people, I will not be a child. That is the way of things. I'll be given a job, and—and a mate, too, I suppose. Though I hadn't thought about that much."

"Really, Oledana?" he teased. "I suspect the mate is exactly what you were thinking of, to be coming out here as you have."

"It's true," she sighed deeply. "If I'm not available for the next harvest, Dolute will end up picking somebody else."

"And who is Dolute?" Anne teased her.

"Only the most gruesome demon ever," she said on a sigh. "His horns are so long—and that wingspread is to die for!"

"And does Dolute know you think this?" she added. "If you really want him to pick you, letting him know would be a good idea."

"It's the first thing I will do when I return," she decided resolutely. "Once I'm declared mature, of course."

"Well then, how about earning that title and finding us some roots?" Harley suggested hopefully.

"Silly fledgling, those things are everywhere," she told him. "You just have to know how to look."

So saying, she tested the density of the ground near the wall of the cave, dug into the soil a bit, and followed a part of a root to its end, breaking off a large chunk. Then she did it twice more, and took them over to the little pool they were near to wash them.

"Yeah, trail mix," Harley cheered as he took his from her. At her strange glance, he said, "It's an Upperworld thing. Means a snack to eat as you hike."

"Oh," she nodded. "Here is your trail mix, friend Anne. I'm very glad you let me come along."

"I'm kind of glad I did, too," she admitted as she rubbed the youngling's head, and then they all set off together.

Chapter Thirty-One

Oledana's wings were starting to ache as she continued to fly behind her companions, but she refused to complain. At least that was what Harley assumed was beginning to slow her pace some time later. He turned to the girl and spoke for the first time in quite a while.

"Why don't you try walking for a while, Oledana, and give your poor wings a rest?" he said. "If you keep on as you are going now, you won't last a day. You should take your modes of travel in turns, since you 've got the advantage of having more than one type."

The young demon smiled at her new friend's thoughtfulness. She had not thought that the fledgling would have given any thought to how easy or hard it was for her to keep up. But then again, if she slowed down it would slow them down as well, for the did not wish to leave her behind.

That was one major difference between the greater and the lesser children of Lilith, she reflected. If she'd been travelling with her own kind, they would leave her behind so she could learn the hard way to keep up. Her people were a practical people, and not given to much emotion. The cheerful banter between them made her appreciate her choice of companions for a first mission even more.

Her stomach began to rumble. That was the only way she knew they must have travelled as long as it took between meals, which was roughly eight hours among her clan. Some other clans ate much more often, but her own clan thought it was too greedy to be so wasteful in a land of limited resources such as they lived in.

"Will we not be eating soon, my friends?" she called to them. "We may have to hunt for meat if you want a full meal."

"We don't have a fire, youngling," Anne pointed out. "And as we are nearing an area where our enemies may well be, it would be most unwise to call attention to ourselves. You'll just have to make do with the roots for now."

"I can't ever remember going without a meal when I was not ill before," Oledana commented. "I don't think my mother would have let me if I'd tried."

"Your mother is not here," Anne reminded her. "Here, we are all in charge of our own lives. You may gather roots when you please, as long as you do not stray far from sight. Else, how would we know if somebody snatched you up right from under our very noses?"

"All right, I will gather us a feast's worth of roots," she announced happily.

"That's a great idea," Anne agreed. "Just remember to stay sharp if you value your hide, okay?"

"Okay," she agreed.

)0(

Although he never would have thought it possible, Harley felt a cool breeze blowing on his face. Looking about curiously, he could find no discernible reason for such a phenomena, but he didn't want Anne to accuse him of being overly analytical again, so he held his peace for a time—until the soft brush of air became a gale force.

"Where on earth is that wind coming from?" he finally asked when he could contain himself no longer.

"There is a vent to the surface somewhere far above—maybe even a series of vents, considering how far beneath the surface we are here. We might be nearing a volcano soon."

"But this wind is cold," Harley pointed out.

"Well, since the ocean isn't spewing water into a pool here, I'd venture to guess it's either pooled somewhere higher up, or this opening is not under water," Anne said. "But we'll know soon enough, if we find water or if we find lava."

"You could figure it out on that map," Harley suggested with a smirk. "It ought to be dry by now."

"Not in front of the youngling," Anne chastised him with a blush.

"Why are you blushing?" Harley teased. "It's not like she knows what I'm talking about."

"That's not true," Oledana told him. "Remember, demons have a much keener sense of smell. Besides, I was lying in wait for the two of you to start your journey."

Had Harley thought Anne was blushing before? Her face went up in flames now as she found herself unable to meet either of their eyes, making both of them burst into laughter.

Anne said, "We should not make so much noise. We're too near the next city, and they are not known to be friends with the vampires."

"But you wear the king's mark," Oledana said in confusion.

"That means very little when we are in a territory where that would mark us immediately as enemies even if our being lesser children did not," Anne pointed out.

"I hadn't thought of that," she said. "Still, we ought to take a break and eat some of these roots."

"We need to find cover from this wind while we rest," Harley added. "It's quite cold here."

"I can see that my vote in the matter will have little pull," said Anne lightly as she looked around for a cave or outcropping for them. Not too distant, a small side cave's opening came into view. "Over there," she said. "That should do nicely."

The three of them went into the small cave and set down their burdens. After eating the small amount of roots

Oledana had already gathered, Anne allowed her to go outside the opening and search for a few more as she and Harley curled up together for a brief nap.

"Remember, though, any sign of movement and you get your butt right back in here, and try to do it without being seen."

"I will," she agreed. "Don't be so worried."

Oledana went out and began digging around. Soon she lost herself in the task, daydreaming about her future. She wondered if Dolute would pick her, or if she would be taken as another demon's mate. With a hopeful sigh, she wished with all her might that such a mate would be worthy of her regard.

So busy with her fantasy that she did not heed Anne's earlier words, Oledana suddenly found herself surrounded by four large demons.

Alarmed greatly, she wondered if perhaps she'd been wishing a bit too hard.

"Look what we have here," said one of them with a rather pleased-sounding growl.

"She looks like she's just about ready to mate," said another with a large grin. He reached out a claw, and it grazed her wingtip, making her pull sharply away.

"Leave me alone!" she gasped.

"Go, deal with her companions," said the obvious leader of the troop. "I will take this one for myself."

The other two demons growled in displeasure at this pronouncement, but the fourth demon bowed and did as he was told without hesitation.

"Did you two have something you wanted to say in the matter?" asked the leader imperiously.

"No, Lodan," they said together. "We cannot hope to win in a battle with you."

Oledana was biting her claw as she simply stared at the quartet in astonishment. She could see no possibility of outrunning them, for she was in complete agreement with the assessment of the others. This Lodan was most definitely a formidable sight. In fact, he put Dolute to shame quite nicely, she realized as she looked him over. Her heart raced with excitement rather than fear, and she wondered what he would do next.

As the others left, he spoke to her. "You are lucky I am here, youngling," he said. "Codar subscribes to the idea that one must beat his mate daily in order to keep her loyal. I find that idea quite ridiculous, myself. What is your name?"

"I am Oledana Jeron," she answered shyly. "I'm on my first adventure."

The large demon smirked indulgently at this. Placing a claw at the nape of her neck and rubbing, he said, "And now it has come to an end. I claim you now for my mate. I believe you will do nicely, pretty one."

Shyly, she bowed her head in submission to this pronouncement. Then, she just had to ask, "Please, I must know. You won't hurt the lesser children, will you? They are on a quest of honor, to stop a murdering feral in the Upperworld. I was hoping they might succeed."

"Do not concern yourself with the cares of the Upperworld, *lialit*," he said as he took her hand. "I want you to concern yourself with other things."

Blushing over his use of the endearment, which translated to "lover", Oledana's hormones went into overdrive at his touch. Oh yes, he was most definitely gruesome! He stroked one of her wingtips as he drew her against him, and then held her to him as he flew away.

Chapter Thirty-Two

Anne awoke with a start just as the three large demons reached the entrance to the small cave, and she sprang to her feet, ready to do battle. Harley got up right behind her, but she put herself between him and their visitors as she cast them a challenging glance.

"Why are you in our territory, lesser?" demanded Codar as he glared at them.

"We are just passing through," Anne said defensively. "There is no way to get where we are going but through this pass."

"And why are you travelling with a youngling?" he wanted to know. "You have not stolen her, have you?"

"Oledana?" she gasped. "What have you done with her?"

"She is no longer your concern," he said imperiously.

"Oledana is far too impetuous for the likes of you," she said. "If she managed to sneak out of her own city to follow us, she could just as easily sneak out of yours."

"The prince has claimed her," he said. "And, by the look and smell of her, I do not think she was adverse to the idea."

"A prince?" said Anne with interest. "That is a very interesting bit of luck for her. It is not my place to speak, of course, and perhaps I need not be so worried over the concerns of my betters, but her mother does not know where she is. I hate to think of how she'd feel if her daughter disappeared with no word. Can she not be told somehow?"

"Why are you being so accepting of this?" Harley inquired in her ear. "Shouldn't you be trying to get her back?"

"That is not the demon way," she whispered. "Plus, the more agreeable we are, the more likely it is they won't kill us right now."

"You will come with us to our city," Codar decided. "The prince is going to want to know more about his new mate. Perhaps she will beg him to spare you, and he'll let you go. He's rather soft-hearted at times. You should be glad of this. If it were me, I'd be serving you up as our next meal."

"Yes, I do believe I'm glad," Anne agreed with a smile of relief. "Will you let us fly freely with you, or must we be chained?"

"Chaining is customary," he answered, rubbing his pointy chin. "But I don't feel like sending Toran to get the things, so you may as well fly free."

"Thank you," said Anne, bowing her head to him. Seeing this, Harley bowed his head as well.

"Yes, thank you," he added, and they all flew off together.

)0(

Lodan took Oledana straight to a large central building at the heart of his city, and flew in through an opening at the top. The room they entered was very comfortable, with a fire burning in a circular hearth in the middle, and a large sleeping area with hides and furs piled up into a comfortable looking bed.

She glanced around, and saw that the eating area was also quite opulent, and she turned to cast him a curious glance.

He chuckled as he watched her, and then he came up behind her, stroking her wings near her back. "Do you know how to cook, youngling?"

"Some things," she answered softly. "I am supposed to have remained with my mother another season, and this would have been the one in which I learned more."

"You are quite intriguing for one who lacks a season," he said, almost on a purr.

"Th-thank you," she answered, feeling a bit nervous now.

Lodan smirked at her tone, and turned her around to face him. "And did she tell you anything about mating, *lialit?*" he asked then. His claws came up around her face on either side, and he stroked down around her ears, making her shiver.

"No," she said. "She believes my mate should tell me those things."

"She is right," he said with a smile. A wise female learns what is expected from her mate, so she will not displease him."

"And wh-what is it you expect?" she asked him, blushing. She could no longer look into his eyes.

Lodan tilted her face up again, and smiled at her. "I'd like to taste you," he answered. "But I suspect your friends are awaiting my decision concerning their lives."

"Must I beg of you?" she inquired softly.

"Why do you care so much?" he asked curiously.

"They have been kind to me," she answered. "They were willing to keep me safe. I wish to do the same for them."

"Then it shall be so," he said. "Come with me, we will tell them together."

"Thank you," she said softly.

"Later, you'll have to make it up to me," he told her with a grin. Then he leaned down and bit her bottom lip. Oledana's reaction was strong and immediate.

"Are you sure that can't be done the other way around?" she inquired, making him chuckle.

"Patience, *lialit*," he said. "You will have much to learn, and I do not like interruptions."

Chapter Thirty-Three

The main hall of Lodan's home was every bit as opulent as his personal chambers. Oledana suspected he must be someone of importance among his people because of the way they behaved around him. When one of them called him *torat* she knew he must be a royal person, yet she still did not know precisely what his status was.

Lodan brought Oledana up to the main dais, where an older demon who was obviously this city's king sat upon his throne looking bored. He looked up when they approached, and then his eyes fell to the young demoness.

"Greetings, father," said Lodan with a smile. "I have found myself a mate this day."

"Who is she?" he inquired, and she knew better than to speak to him before he addressed her, so she remained silent.

"Her name is Oledana Jeron," he said, smiling down at her. She blushed under the perusal of the two demons, who seemed to be waiting for her to speak, yet she was uncertain about the customs here and did not want to anger the king, so still she remained silent.

"Ah, Jeron clan," the king said. "That is a few days march from here, is it not? Where did you find her?"

"She appears to have joined an adventure she deems worthy," he said, winking at her. "Her companions wore the mark of her king, but I suspect she did not have permission to leave the city with them."

"Is that true, girl?"

Finally, Oledana thought, relieved to have her permission at last. "I am supposed to have remained with my mother one more season, yet my companions are kind, and their quest is just, so I followed them even after they'd instructed me to remain. I really believe they are going to need help to achieve their goals."

"And you, Lodan, will you heed the words of your new mate, or are you just as silly as your brothers?"

"What do you mean?" Lodan asked. "I do not intend to beat her, if that's what you are asking."

"I wondered if you intend to help her," he answered with an indulgent smile. "You know how well my new mate and I get along. I believe it is mostly because I was willing to listen to her as well as command."

"Is this so?" he answered curiously.

"Oledana Jeron, what is the quest of the two vampires who so recently were brought into the hall?" the king inquired, indicating the pair who were seated with the three demons she'd seen earlier at one of the lower tables. "I must admit, I had thought to destroy them until Codar told me the decision belonged to my son."

Nervous now, knowing she held Anne and Harley's lives in her hands, she answered, "It is a most noble undertaking, sire. They wish to stop a killer from harming more Upperworld people. I know that these people are nothing to us, but the two of them seemed very concerned by the feral vampire's behavior. And also, I believe their hearts are in the right place. I would not wish to see them killed out of hand."

"Have the vampires brought forth," said the king. "I would like to witness this nobility of which you speak."

Lodan held up a hand and the other demons brought forth the captives. "Ah, I see they've left you in one piece. That is all to the good."

Anne and Harley both bowed their heads to the royals, wisely remaining silent.

"They are unchained?" asked the king, surprised. "You, too, must have felt this pair to be worthy of trust, to have left them thus."

"They gave no reason for us to believe they would cause trouble," Codar answered with a slight bow. "It is most unusual, sire. But then again, these are difficult times."

"Difficult?" the king scoffed, raising one brow.

"Difficult, how?" Oledana whispered to Lodan, who softly put a finger to her lips as the king and the other demon continued their talking.

"My son has claimed your little demoness," said the monarch to the vampires. "It is her belief that you are worthy of her help, so I must ask you this. Why is your quest so important, and what would you give in exchange for my letting you live?"

"I suppose to you the deaths of a few humans means little," Harley said. "But until recently, I was one of those humans, and I made a vow to protect and serve. I know that now that I'm a vampire that will mean little to my future, but I cannot willingly walk away from my past with a fellow vampire still rampaging among them, killing them with such violence. With modern means of blood extraction, their deaths need never occur."

"So you wish to honor a word-bond to protect others from this feral creature?" he asked. "And what will you do, once you have fulfilled this duty? Surely you will not continue your loyalties beyond this act?"

"I hadn't given it much thought," he admitted. "I wanted to plan that after I survived the upcoming ordeal, I suppose. I would not wish to make such a plan and then be unable to enact it."

"You are wise," the king said. "I have decided that my son and his new mate shall accompany you on your journey. When your task is complete, I will expect you to return to this place to serve whatever purpose I decide to have you fulfill. Is that agreeable?"

"I will do as I can" he answered, glancing over at Anne, who nodded her head in confirmation of his words.

"Father, you wish me to help the lesser children?" Lodan clarified. "I thought you wanted to eradicate that breed."

"Only the parts of it that lack compassion," he answered. "I see what you all have seen as I watch them. They are indeed on a worthy mission. Oh yes, and before I forget, Happy birthday, and good job on finding your mate so fast."

"Thank you, sire," he said. "I will endeavor to do my best in both love and war, as always. Oledana and I will see all of you later, however. We have other matters to attend to."

The rest of them chuckled, and the young demoness blushed and could not meet any of their eyes. Lodan scooped her up in his arms and flew off with her again.

Chapter Thirty-Four

Anne and Harley were given a large bedchamber somewhere in the castle to wait out the ardor of a newly mated demonic pair, and were currently snuggled together on a large pile of leathers and furs near their own open hearth. On the very top of the pile, they had the map spread open to read.

"Well, we can cut off some of the journey since we'll have the prince along," she said, running her finger down the new path they'd be able to take."

"But look, Anne, that takes us right by a lake of fire," Harley pointed out. "I'm not so sure I want to get up close and personal with all that molten lava."

"I thought you liked getting up close and personal to hot things," she teased him, grinning broadly.

"Imp," he said, tweaking her nose. Then his hand went underneath her chin, drawing her in for a kiss. He hadn't planned on its intensity being quite so heated, but apparently his woman had more in mind than just cuddling.

Her soft groan both confirmed this and fired him up as well all at the same time. With mutual unspoken consent, they laid right on top of the map, not without giggling as they did so, and proceeded to explore.

"What is it about this map, anyway?" Harley teased her.

"I like to go all the way?" she suggested, and they laughed again.

Harley sat up and pulled off his shirt, and then took hers off as well. Each of them removed the rest of their clothes and got comfortable again. Harley found his comfortable spot with his head between her thighs, and Anne found this position looked rather promising.

"Don't forget the right turn at Albuquerque," she said, and made him laugh just as his tongue had found her sweet slit.

"Did you want to do this, or would you rather tell knock-knock jokes?" he inquired, licking her several times as he did so.

"If you knock, I can open the door," she chuckled.

"Knock-knock," he said.

"Who's there?"

"Orange."

"Orange who?" she asked, giggling again.

"Orange you glad I have a banana?" he answered, then moved over her and slid right in.

"Hell, yes," she replied, moving right along with him as he set the pace, neither fast nor slow, but just right for making her squeal with need and wrap her legs around his thighs. "Oh yes, make me come, Harley. That's so damn good!"

Her clenching walls felt too good to resist, and soon the well sated pair fell, twined together, in the middle of the map again, drifting off to sleep.

)0(

Several hours later, the demon couple and the vampire couple met in the Great Hall, casting each other knowing and rather satisfied smiles as they went in together before the king.

"Father, we have returned to prepare for the journey," Lodan announced as they all approached the dais, everyone but the prince bowing slightly as they arrived.

"Ah, very good," he answered. "I don't suppose I need to remind you to be careful, and return to me in one piece? I'd hate to have spent the last seventy seasons raising you only to get you killed right as you've finally become your own demon."

"I am far too happy just now to allow anything to kill me off," he commented, his eyes going over to his new mate of their own accord before he schooled his features again.

"She does look like a most satisfactory prize," he said softly, looking into his son's eyes.

"Apparently," he said as mildly as he could. The king barked out a laugh, and gave his shoulder a squeeze just in front of the place where the wing joined—a mark of affection among their kind reserved only for their closest family and mates. "It does not appear I'll need another to go with her," he added a bit louder, so she could hear him.

Oledana blushed and looked down at her claws, which she held clasped together in front of her. Lodan chucked her under the chin so she would look at him, then winked at her. She smiled up into his eyes, clearly affected by the touch.

"Your supplies are packed and waiting near the gate," the king said. "I wish you all a good journey, and much fortune in reaching your goal."

"Thank you, Your Majesty," Anne and Harley answered as one.

Oledana cast the king a shy smile and did not speak, and Lodan wrapped an arm about her waist to bring her along as the others led the way back down and out of the building. The chill of the blowing winds immediately hit them all as they headed back toward the exit to the city.

"Is it always so cold here?" Oledana asked Lodan curiously. "I've never actually felt wind before, though I was told of its existence."

"I will keep you warm each night, *lialit*," he answered. "Though I suppose for now, we ought to dress warm for this leg. Don't you think so too, my new friends?"

"Vampires are a bit more resistant to the cold than most," Anne said. "But it never hurts to dress warm, so we don't have to resist to begin with."

"Hear, hear!" Harley chimed in agreement.

When they'd reached the gate and obtained their packs, each of them brought out the warm fur cloaks they found inside, and wrapped themselves into them. They had sashes to tie them in place, so their hands could remain comfortably free.

Lodan and Harley each solicitously tied the sashes onto their females, and each received a kiss to the side of the neck independent of one another. Both males laughed as they realized they'd simultaneously done this.

"Hey, this is supposed to be an adventure, not a honeymoon," Anne grumbled.

"But it is a honeymoon," Harley pointed out. "You and I haven't been together much longer than they have. It's inevitable."

"Yes, I suppose so," Anne conceded. "But for now, let us get some distance under our feet. This journey is taking more time than I like so far."

"Always the sensible slave driver," he teased as he kissed her again. "But she does have a point."

"Yes," Lodan agreed. "Let us be away at once."

So each of them picked up a pack, and they all wandered out into the craggy rocks that littered the ground outside the pillars, and headed east at a steady clip, each couple's hands joined as they went.

Chapter Thirty-Five

"We are fast approaching the territory of the worst fiends of the Underdwell," Lodan mentioned several hours later. "They kill everyone indiscriminately, but they have an especial dislike for lesser children and those who would choose to associate with them. We must tread with care and quiet here."

The others nodded at his words, and they moved more cautiously as they hid behind stalagmites wherever possible. Oledana wanted desperately to ask how long they would have to do this, but she knew better than attempt to ask.

Anne, seeing her frustrated expression, leaned over and gave her shoulder a little squeeze, which caused Lodan to momentarily raise his brow. He knew that the vampire had a soft spot for the girl, yet it irritated him slightly to see such intimacy between them.

Harley, who was oblivious to the exchange and its nuances, continued walking with a look of determined concentration that broke the tension between the prince and the vampire female almost as soon as it had begun. They both smirked as they watched him move, and shrugged at each other.

Oledana had seen the smirks between Anne and Lodan, and begun to feel jealous at their apparent comradery. She had completely missed the fact that the pair had had any momentary clashing where she was concerned. So as she walked, she wondered why the pair would have a need to think of each other when they each had someone else along.

This line of thinking had her tensed up, and then she felt Lodan's claw-tips slide down the edge of her lower wing and reclaim the place on her shoulder where the other female had touched, lingering there as they walked. She wanted to still nurture the jealousy that had welled up inside her, but found it impossible to do so with the rapid beating of her heart keeping her from having any coherent thought at all.

Suddenly Harley froze up ahead. They'd been walking over an hour in the midst of the rocky outcroppings and pointed stalactites and stalagmites without any problems. However, it looked like they were about to face their first difficulty.

As Lodan reached Harley's side, he set his mate behind him to shield her from any harm, and Anne brought up the rear, her eyes ever-watching for anything that tried to approach from behind.

"*Scaolan!*" she whispered urgently, and Lodan turned in time to see the loan enemy scout rounding a stalagmite, still unaware he'd found anything amiss.

So quick Anne barely perceived his movement even with her vampire eyes, Lodan broke off a stalactite from above and hurled it with deadly accuracy at the other demon, skewering him before he had any chance to sound an alarm. Anne thought this quite clever, for if the others in his troop did find him, they'd just assume the roof of the cave had dropped on of its teeth upon him, rather than realize the true origin.

"There's a cave ahead," Harley whispered, waving them all forward.

One at a time, each creeped across the open area between themselves and the cave, Harley, then Anne, then Oledana, and lastly Lodan, who would be the most noticeable should they be spotted. When he, too, had made it across, only then did the others duck inside the hiding place.

"I will see if there's a way out of here," said Anne softly, and she scurried off on her private mission.

"It's hot in here," Oledana whispered as she loosed the fur at her throat a bit.

"Hush, *lialit*," Lodan reminded her as he pulled her against his chest. She could feel how rapidly his heart was beating, and she knew that this time she was not the cause.

Anne returned, looking very concerned, but she motioned the others to follow her anyway.

When they were much farther into the cave, she voiced her misgivings. "This whole area is littered with fire pools," she told them. "I don't think we're going to like where we come out, but I'm at least certain that we will, since I can feel a breeze from the other side."

"A very hot breeze," Lodan pointed out with concern. Pulling his mate to him again, he reached down and untied the sash holding her furs in place, and slid the clothing item off of her, copping a feel of her breast as he did so.

Oledana thrilled to the touch even as she felt the infectious fear that mirrored in everyone else's eyes. She was no fool. Where there was heat, there must be a reason for it. She turned in Lodan's arms and untied his sash as well, then took both cloaks and their sashes, and tucked them into their packs.

"Should we rest a bit before we go on?" Harley asked uncertainly.

"Hold, let me listen," Lodan said then, and everyone froze as he did so. "They are within the cave. We'll have to press on now, and with a quickness."

"Damn!" Harley grumbled. It was a sentiment shared by all. As they reached the far end of the cave, it opened out over a huge lake of fire with no way around except over the top in flight.

"I will carry you," said Lodan as he took Oledana into his arms protectively.

"You'll have enough trouble carrying yourself," she said firmly. "I must do this on my own. I don't need you to baby me like my mother always did. How am I to prove my worth if I'm never allowed to try?"

"This is a dangerous place to first spread your wings," he told her, the concern on his face quite clear.

"Still, I will do it," she insisted.

Lodan let her go, and the vampires each sprouted a pair of wings. Even as they began to fly, they could hear the enemy demons approaching in the caves. Unaware of the presence of the four, they were making no attempt at stealth.

"Look!" shouted one as the four adventurers began to fly out over the heated pool. The other demons who were with him came running as well.

"No matter," said one of them. "No one has ever managed to fly all the way across that pool. Just let them go to their deaths."

This pronouncement was heard by the young Oledana with some degree of concern. She was finding it difficult already to keep up with the others.

The heat beneath her hit her in agonizing waves, and she flew a bit higher in hopes of avoiding it. Much higher, however, and she'd be hindered by the stalactites instead. Speed was the only answer, and she did not seem to be in possession of it.

Lodan's arms were suddenly around her, and she folded in her wings, accepting what he'd already known to be true. This time, at least, she needed help. It was not much longer before she fainted from the heat, hanging limply as he shuttled her the rest of the way.

Chapter Thirty-Six

When Oledana opened her eyes she found herself lying on a fur beside Lodan, who was fast asleep. Glancing at his forearm, she saw that he'd been badly burned, and someone had bandaged him up. Imagining Anne doing the bandaging, a pang of jealousy went through her before she could force herself to stop it.

She sighed as she laid on her back and gazed up at the smooth surface of the ceiling above. Wherever they were, they'd left the pointed stalactites behind, at the very least. She'd hated the things always looking so formidably and threatening above them.

At any time one could break loose and skewer whoever happened to be below. She had, of course, lived with that fact all her life, but far fewer stalactites existed in her childhood home. The long expanse they'd just passed through had been a much deadlier place.

She padded over to a discrete place and relieved herself, looking over at her companions even as she did so. It was strange to realize that in so short a time she'd gone from a carefree child to an adventuring adolescent to a mated female.

What would her mother say to it all when she discovered what she'd done? Would she be furious at her temerity, or would she perhaps be pleased by her apparent success? After all, she had just been mated to a prince, hadn't she.

And what a handsome prince he was, she added, hugging herself. She hadn't known what to expect when it came to mating, but Lodan had proven to be a tender lover, and she looked forward to the time he would touch her again.

So busy fantasizing about him that she didn't even see him get up, she opened her eyes as he took a hand and pulled her up into his arms.

"Are you sleeping over here?" he teased her.

"Of course not," she answered, though she realized afterwards that she might have been. "I merely needed to go—"

"Hush," he said softly. "Don't wake the others. I want to touch you."

He leaned down and brushed one of his horns along the side of her face, making her quiver slightly. Boldly, Oledana did it back, pleased when he was unable to contain his groan of surprise.

"*Lialit,*" he breathed. "I'll race you to that cave."

)0(

As soon as he saw the two demons depart, Harley chuckled and leaned over top of Anne's sleeping form, kissing her cheek, her eat, and then the side of her neck. She awakened with a pleased little moan and wrapped her arms around him.

"We appear to be alone," he said, rather pleased by this idea.

"Really?" she asked, smiling up at him with interest. "Where'd they go?"

"There's a little cave a ways up the path," he answered. "I think we can safely assume they won't return for a while. Would you like to take advantage of the fact, my dear?"

Instead of answering him with words, Anne leaned forward and bit the side of his neck, letting a little blood trickle over her lips and tongue. Harley groaned at the pleasurable sensation, reveling in her touch.

"Take me, Harley," she encouraged him, her voice laced with reckless abandon.

They both heard Oledana's pleased gasp from within the cave, and smiled. Harley did not waste time with unclothing either of them, instead opting for uncovering the pertinent areas just enough to make use of them. He slid deep into Anne's heated folds, and she, too, gave a pleased gasp as pleasure racked her body.

The sounds of the other couple's lovemaking merely heightened their own pleasure, so that they moved with more and more zeal, coming blissfully together, and then holding each other close.

"Hey, we forgot the map," said Harley some time later. Both of them burst into mirthful giggles just as the demons were headed back.

"What is so funny?" Lodan inquired as he allowed his mate to leave his side and set about straightening the fur they were about to lay down on again.

"Oh, nothing," Anne answered. "I was just telling Harley I thought we could use a compass."

Harley laughed again and swatted Anne's backside.

"I do not think they work the same down here," Lodan said in all seriousness. "Are not your poles different up there?"

"I don't think our poles are all that different," she answered, trying not to laugh. Harley, however, was not making it easy as he snickered in the background.

"Have you two been reading maps again?" asked Oledana innocently, knowing full well that Lodan would not catch the reference and they would.

"Yes, yes we have," Harley answered, schooling his features. "It was most—educational."

Lodan could tell they were not talking about what they seemed to be, and cast all his companions a curious glance. "What's so funny about reading maps and using compasses?" he wanted to know.

"Nothing," Anne said with a smirk. "Nothing at all."

Chapter Thirty-Seven

The following day found the intrepid couples hiding just outside the gates of Fagon. The males were peeking over the rise while the females hovered behind them. Harley and Lodan slid back down to confer with their mates.

"I don't want to risk inquiring at the gates," Harley told Anne. "I don't seem to think that was how I got in the last time. I think there is a cave that will take us beneath the city. I just wish I could remember where it was."

"Follow your instincts, my dear," she said. "Let your mind rest, and listen to your body instead. It may remember what your brain does not."

On Anne's advice, Harley allowed himself to clear his mind, and allowed his body to simply go where it willed. He led the others several miles away from the gate, even to the point they began to wonder if he was daft, when suddenly they found an opening in the solid rock.

"This is it," Harley exclaimed. "I'm certain of it."

"Let's go in," Lodan said in agreement.

All in accord, they stepped through the hole and found themselves in a small antechamber. At one end of the room glowed a huge blue portal, very inviting. At the other end was another portal of a fiery red. It looked likely to incinerate anything it touched, leaving them all wary of it.

"A portal," Anne said happily, starting to move toward the blue light.

"Not that one," Harley cautioned her. "That one is a trap. It leads somewhere most unpleasant, to say the least."

"Are you sure, Harley?" she asked in surprise.

"We're in the Underdwell, remember?" he pointed out. "Of course there will be a preference for fire down here."

"I guess that true," she said, glancing at the demons uncertainly.

"He is quite correct," Lodan assured her. "We must take the red portal."

"Very well, then," she said with some misgivings. "Let us go."

Lodan stepped forward immediately, took Oledana by the hand, and the two of them stepped through together. Casting Anne a glance of reassurance, Harley also stepped right through the glowing red portal and disappeared from view.

Biting her lower lip, Anne stepped to the portal so that she was inches away from entering, and stood contemplating her choice.

Without warning, the portal pulsed, sucking her into it. She closed her eyes tightly as she was flung shakily about for several seconds before she alit on solid rock once more. Taking in her surroundings, she felt disappointed by the normal-looking rocks and dirt surrounding her.

"What's that sound?" she asked after a few moments. "It sounds like moaning."

"I do believe we're in a bit of trouble," Lodan pointed out. "I distinctly smell undead human flesh. We are near at least ten zombies—maybe more."

"Maybe a lot more," Oledana mentioned as she stared at the pack of zombies who were just entering through the mouth of a small cave nearby. "Time to leave."

Flapping her wings, Oledana shot upwards about ten feet and hovered there, wondering why her companions didn't do the same. Lodan reached up and pulled her down by her foot. She let him take her into his arms so she could hear what he had to say.

"You shouldn't fly, Oledana," he said. "They'll be able to see you. We'd rather not alert the guards of this gate to our presence, as it's the one we're trying to get past."

"Then what do we do about them?" she wanted to know as the group of zombies began muttering amongst themselves, and she distinctly heard the word 'brains' out of more than one. "Fast, get up to the top of the hill and over the other side," Harley instructed.

"What about the guards at the gate?" Lodan protested. They're sure to see us."

"We won't be going through the gate," Harley told him. "We would never make it in alive, trying any gate."

"Then where are we going?"

"Right now, we're going up and over that hill," Harley insisted.

Oledana yelped as one of the zombies gripped her wrist. Lodan punched its face in and reclaimed his woman without even batting an eye, and flew the two of them up and over the hill just as the vampire had suggested. Trouble was, more zombies appeared to be on the other side.

"I believe your plan has a bit of a flaw, vampire," he commented wryly. "There's at least twenty more of our newfound friends over here."

"Damn!" Harley cursed under his breath. "Just stay up there. I don't think they'll try to climb up. Come on, Anne," he added as he grabbed her hand and they both scrambled up to the top as well."

"Isn't this cozy?" Anne commented with her most brilliant smile.

"Quite," Lodan agreed as he pulled Oledana into his lap and held her close.

"I don't suppose they'll just leave," Harley commented ruefully.

"Probably not," Lodan told him. "But there are plenty of rocks up here to pitch at them. Might be a good time for some target practice."

Harley chuckled and said, "I'll let you do the honors. You're probably much better at it than I am."

Lodan grabbed a few rocks and sadistically began picking off zombies.

He was careful to aim for the eyes, hoping to blind them since he couldn't hope to hack their heads off their bodies with rocks from fifty feet away.

"Too bad we don't have a sword or something," he said after a while. "I could go down there and eliminate the whole problem in short order."

"Remind me to bring a sword on my next adventure, will you, Anne?" Harley said to her with a slight smirk.

"Would a dagger do, by any chance?" Anne asked the demon prince. "I found one in my pack earlier."

"Why didn't you say so?" he asked, feeling better already. "Back in a thrice."

The others watched as Lodan sprang to life. He swooped down on the assembly below and started slicing, his deadly blows quickly doing enough damage to equal that of ten men.

"That's pretty impressive," Harley pointed out.

"Yes, it is," Oledana agreed with a wicked smile gracing her face. It was as much sadistic as it was aroused.

"Well, it gets the job done," said Anne briskly. "Now all we have to do is bypass the gate and its guards and find some way inside. No problem."

Harley made a face that said otherwise. "Problem?"

"We're going to have to look for another cave," he said. "But don't worry, it won't be any different than looking for the first."

"Well, if you don't count the fact these caves are crawling with those freaks," Anne pointed out. "Yeah, like I said. Should be no problem at all."

"Not with my mate around, anyway," Oledana announced proudly, making the other two smile. They chose to leave that pride intact—at least for the time being.

Chapter Thirty-Eight

About an hour later, and a few zombie battles under their belts, the quartet found the other cave opening. The main problem with this was that they also found about twenty more zombies blocking the path.

"Not again," Anne said with a sigh.

"They haven't spotted us," Harley said. "Maybe we could wait a bit and they'll just wander off."

"Yeah, and the Pope is an Irishman," she commented.

"Is he? I don't keep up with that sort of thing."

"Funny," she said with an insincere smile.

"We're all pretty tired," Harley said. "It'd be a good idea to rest up before going into yet another unknown situation. At least if we rest here, we already know what we've got to contend with."

"He does have a point." Lodan added. "Besides, my wrists are starting to ache from all the stabbing."

"We should take the cave first, and then block the opening somehow," said Anne. "It'd at least be safer than staying out in the open."

"Please, I'm just too tired to bother with the damned zombies yet," Harley said grumpily. "We've been at this for hours now, Anne. I could really use a break."

"You sound like it," she told him. "What do you two think?"

"I think we could find a spot to rest nearby," Lodan said as he took in Harley's tense shoulders and slightly disheveled hair, both traits the vampire usually never possessed. "After all, we're about to get to the important bit."

"Yes, I agree, too," Oledana said tiredly. "Most of us are not used to so much exercise in one day."

Anne finally realized she was being argumentative because she, too, was exhausted. "It won't do any harm to rest a bit," she decided. "But not too long, mind you. We're in a lot of danger in this place."

"You don't have to tell us that twice," Harley agreed as he ambled over to a huge rock pile and found a place to hide in it. The others followed suit, and soon they were all sitting among the rocks, halfway asleep.

"I figured out why we're so tired, Harley," Anne said then as she pulled out the blood thermos and pushed the button to heat it. "This is the last of it, so we'd better enjoy it while we can."

As the two finished their meal, the familiar sound that had been plaguing them all this time met their ears yet again. "Brains!" a zombie moaned, and entered their little encampment. Several others came in from other openings, and they realized with a sinking feeling that this attack must have been somewhat organized, despite the stupid appearance of their attackers.

"You can't be serious," Anne grumbled as she sprang to her feet, prepared to do battle again. "This is getting old so fast."

"Tell me about it," Harley agreed.

"That's it, I've had enough," she announced. "I'm going into that cave, and I'm going to take the blue portal, and that's final. You all can do as you like, but I'm out of here."

The others watched in astonishment as she sprouted wings and flew right out of the battle and headed straight for the cave. Harley cast his companions an uncertain look.

"If they all came here, they won't be there," Lodan pointed out.

"Well then, what are we waiting for?" Harley said. "I've got to stop Anne from entering the blue gate."

"What's so bad about the blue gate?" he inquired.

"I can't remember," he admitted. "I just seem to think it's something bad, like we're not supposed to go there."

"Is that from a memory, or is it a feeling you got just as you approached the caves?" Lodan prompted.

"When I approached, I guess," he told him.

"It's a compelling charm," Lodan told him with some certainty. "They put it on the blue gateway so we wouldn't use it. I think your lady must somehow be immune. I believe it would be best to follow her lead."

Offhandedly, as if it were just an everyday task, Lodan plunged his dagger into a zombie's eye without even bothering to look at it. He watched Harley instead for some sign the vampire had made a decision.

"Well, it makes about as much sense as anything else," he agreed as he turned to bash a zombie's skull. "No point staying here, either way."

"You've got that right," Lodan agreed as he stepped over to Oledana's side and stabbed her attacker a bit more fiercely than he had his own. "Come, *lialit*, let us leave this place. I'm as tired of it as they are."

"Sounds good to me," she said as she took his hand. The three of them flew up and over the zombies, and discovered there were over fifty of them vying for a chance to get through the cracks.

They landed at the cave entrance and stepped inside.

The place looked so similar to the last one that they began to think it actually was the same cave, and only the surroundings had changed.

They arrived just in time to see Anne walk right up to the blue portal and step in, disappearing from view. One by one, the trio followed her into the abyss.

Chapter Thirty-Nine

They found themselves at the heart of the city, surrounded by a few surprised guards who looked as though they weren't sure what to do. Their apparent leader stepped forward.

"Did you know of this entrance, or have you happened here by chance?" he demanded menacingly.

"We seek the Necromancer," Harley said with authority. "I am a former acolyte, come to seek more of his teachings. Both he and I have swapped a few lifetimes, but I think he should be able to remember my soul."

"Outsiders have no business in Fagon," he said as he attempted to stare

Harley down. "The punishment for entry is usually death."

"I am a member of the mage guild here," Harley told him.

"The mage guild was abolished a century ago," he countered.

"Where is the Necromancer?" Harley demanded at his most imperious. "He surely will wish to welcome me home."

"The Necromancer is unfortunately a young child at the moment," he sneered. "I doubt he can help you."

"How old is he?" Harley asked, somewhat deflated.

"He is only three," the man told him.

"Great! Now what do we do?" he asked his friends.

Anne stepped forward and said, "You'll have to dream with him, of course."

"You want me to try my first dream seek in this body with a three year old?" he asked.

"I will go with you, Harley," she said serenely. "The information we seek is still within him. You there, guard, you must bring us to a sleeping place. Our need is too great to await the Necromancer's maturity."

"I don't know if you've noticed, but you haven't been welcomed to the city as yet," he pointed out.

"Well then take us to whoever it is that welcomes people to the city so we can tend to the business for which we've come," she said, exasperated by his dense behavior in a city famed for its intelligence.

"There's a problem with that, too," he answered uncomfortably. "We haven't got anyone that does that at the moment. We've been ordered to kill everyone, so there's not been a need."

"Well, that's stupid," Anne told him.

"I—I'm not sure how to deal with this."

"How about you just put us somewhere so we can go to sleep and seek the soul of the Necromancer?" said Harley as if it should be obvious. "It can't be that difficult to do."

"Well, perhaps we can put you up till we hold a meeting?" he said uncertainly. "This sort of issue hasn't come up in our lifetimes. We shouldn't just kill you out of hand. If you'll just follow me, I'll take you to the old sanatorium. There are many open rooms to be had in there."

"You have no senate?" Anne gasped. "How are you running a city here at all?"

"That's a good question," he said. "We really haven't been running one at all."

They followed him to the center of the city proper, which was quite large and quite littered with unkempt remains of garbage and excrement. The smell was terrible, so that they had to hold their noses at times.

"Here is the building that once housed the mighty senate," he said dejectedly. "They were a thousand strong, and they were great. How far the mighty Fagon has fallen."

"But what has happened here?" Harley wanted to know. "Why has Fagon fallen so low?"

"I believe it is because we resisted change too much," he said. "We remained in the Dark Ages while the rest of the world moved ahead without us. All greatness is only great if it is maintained."

"That is probably the truest statement I've ever heard," Harley agreed.

"Go on in, find a place to stay if you can," he said. "And be careful of the citizens. They'll eat you as soon as look at you. The crops haven't fared well over the years either."

"That's even better news," Harley said, casting Anna a pointed look.

"We'll go to the archives," she said. "Maybe we can find something in there."

"Maybe we should fly?" Lodan suggested, though until that point he had deigned to remain apart from the proceedings. It was the vampires' quest, after all. He and his mate were just along for the ride.

"No, it is too difficult in the labyrinthine infrastructure," Anne told him. "We're just going to have to walk."

"You sound as though you've been in there before," the guard commented.

"I have," she said. "But that was a very long time ago."

"Well, then, let's be off," he said. "We're not going to find anyplace to get some rest standing out here."

"Oh, by the way, heads up," said the guard as he turned to go. "They like to lie in wait just inside the doors."

"Thanks for the info," Lodan said, readying his weapon with a grin. "I was starting to think things were about to get boring."

The four of them stepped inside the huge stone doorway and began to make their way across the large courtyard. Because they'd fallen into the habit with all the zombies, they easily fell into the same one again, with each one's eyes trained on one corner as they all walked forward. So far, so good.

"They're probably inside the structure itself," Lodan said. "Keep watching."

"Shit, they're above us," Harley said as he caught a glimpse of someone right before he leapt down on him. Baring his fangs, Harley surged forward and fell upon him, making a meal of him instead of the other way around.

Other people fell down upon them. With no time to bother counting, they all set to maiming and killing instead. Anne had a moment to say, "If you bite them, Harley, make sure they're dead. We are not here to make new vampires."

"Good idea," he agreed, and they broke apart again.

For almost an hour they fought their way to the door with no idea if another fight lay just inside. They killed so many people they had to step on the bodies as the continued to fight the foes who still remained.

"Hey, assholes, if you're so hungry, just eat the ones we killed,"

Harley shouted. "Why do you want us to kill you all?" Not long after this pronouncement, many of the combatants started to drag away the dead, leaving the fight behind. "Damn! Should have thought of that sooner," he said, and the four of them all headed for the door.

Chapter Forty

"What is this place," asked Lodan as they stepped inside the archive hall. Scrolls lined every wall, each stored in its own slot. More scrolls were stored in long, tall shelves for as far as the eye could see."

"This is by far the greatest receptacle of knowledge that has ever existed," Anne told them with reverent awe. "It's also one pain in the ass to find what you're looking for in here because they've got it all written in Sanskrit and Latin. Too bad they couldn't pick one or the other. Makes it harder to figure out what you're looking at sometimes."

"I can only read the Latin, unfortunately," Lodan admitted.

"What, why would a demon learn Latin?" Harley wanted to know.

"It's what the scribes down here use to communicate," he explained. "Since we are a warlike race, and I am meant to go out and fight, it is always a good idea to be able to read the communications being passed between our potential enemies."

"Yeah, I guess that makes sense," he agreed.

"Harley, I need you to sleep," Anne told him, uncovering a long, wide desk that was littered with papers. "It's your job to try to reach the mind of the Necromancer, see what you can find out."

"I thought you were going to come with?" he inquired.

"I will come in after a while," she said. "When I know that you are fully asleep and seem to be communicating."

Before he could protest further, she ran her hand over his forehead, and he felt a wave of pure exhaustion hit him. Irritated, he cast her an annoyed look. "I don't need to be compelled by my maker, woman. I'll go to sleep on my own."

"There's no time for stubbornness now, my love," she insisted as she ran her hand over his forehead yet again. Harley was asleep before he could say another word about it. She caught him and laid him down on the desk.

"He's going to be mad when he wakes up," Lodan commented with a smirk.

"I'll make it up to him," she commented dryly.

"I'm sure you will," he chuckled, then turned to see a slight scowl marring Oledana's pretty face as she watched them. "My little *lialit*, have you learned any Latin by any chance?"

"No," she answered, feeling useless.

He gave her an encouraging smile, and said, "Then I suppose you'd better guard the entrance. We don't want any extra company getting in here. If you see anything out of the ordinary, you must sound the alarm at once. I don't want to lose you right after I just obtained you to begin with."

"I will," she agreed, and glided a claw along the side of his face before she turned away and headed for the door they'd come in. It had holes in it so she could see out into the corridor beyond. At the moment, it was blissfully clear of anyone.

Anne wasted no time looking for some kind of document or other tool that was used to organize the vast array of documents before them. If they incorporated any sort of an alphanumerical system to find things, they'd be able to obtain what they wanted with much greater ease.

"I will begin to browse," Lodan said. "Tell me specifically what it is you want, so I'll know it if I see it."

"There is a necromantic spell used to bind an eternal soul from doing harm," she explained. "It is that spell, and the knowledge required to cast it properly, which we seek. If we are lucky, Harley will simply get it out of the child. But it never hurts to have a back-up plan."

"I never knew vampires were so wise," he commented dryly. "I was always taught to abhor them."

"I am a very old vampire, and a child of one of the original children," she said. "Not all vampires are as old or as wise as the old ones like me. It is a gift from Mother Lilith that seems to be diluted when a vampire is made instead of bred."

"And your mate?"

"He is a made vampire," she admitted. "But he is quite wise for such a one. I did not know that the souls of humans possessed a great knowledge and power of their own. The combination within him is exactly what is needed to stop the feral."

"Tell me something, Vivianne le Fade, child of true vampires," Lodan said. "Why are you so attached to this fledgling?"

"He has great power, though he does not remember this," she explained. "He was a sorcerer and necromancer when he was first turned, and had that knowledge still when first we came together. I was already tracking the feral back then, but the task was given to him instead, and so it is his to finish.

But still I will help him all I can, for my heart is his. I knew the moment I saw him I'd be his forever."

"Forever?" Lodan asked with a smile. "A rather romantic notion."

"We possess an undying fire," she excused herself with a small smile. "Now, get to browsing, demon prince who has so romantically attached himself to a youngling at the mere first sight of her. Do you not think I can see your fire as well?"

With a bark of appreciation, Lodan nodded. "So it is," he agreed, and turned to his task without another word. He moved methodically through the shelves even as Anne sifted methodically through the papers that had littered the desk as she watched Harley sleep.

Within his dream, Harley came upon a small boy playing in a box of sand. "Master?" he said as he sat down with him there.

"Where have you been? Don't you know we have work to do?" said the boy with a stern frown as he looked up at him. "Getting yourself killed has set us back centuries, Oleuth. Now, what do you remember?"

"Nothing much, I'm sorry to say," he admitted. "I've been reborn several times, and in a few of my incarnations, including this one, I've even been a vampire myself."

"Did you plan to die again, then?" he inquired curiously.

"No, I have a mate," he said dismissively. "Now, about the feral. I must relearn how to bind him, Master. He has been killing again."

"That is no great surprise," he said with a sage grin that seemed strange on the face of such a young child. Far too knowing, and yet youthfully innocent at the same time.

"Come, Oleuth, enter my memories," he invited. "All shall be revealed within."

Chapter Forty-One

"Why can't I seem to sleep," Anne grumbled as she ran her hand down Harley's face again. It was obvious he was with the ancient mage, and yet somehow she was unable to enter into a sleep state to join them. "Perhaps the old man is keeping me out. Why would he want to do that?"

It was quite disconcerting to think that a mere three year old would disallow an ancient vampire from communing with it. More and more, Anne was finding that humans were a much more resilient and intelligent breed than she gave them credit for. It was almost like the prejudices of greater children against lesser was too similar to the prejudices of the lesser children to the sons and daughters of Eve.

"This is getting me nowhere," she finally growled as she sat up and renewed her search for a cataloguing system. Ironically, she discovered the scroll with the key to the organization within a minute of renewing her attempts. She'd been trying to fall asleep using it as her pillow, as a matter of fact.

"That was just too convenient," she grumbled, and went to join Lodan and tell him where they ought to be looking.

A commotion broke out by the entrance, and Oledana's voice rang out as she shouted and lunged forward to attack an intruder. When she saw the door had been opened by a small child, she hesitated in mid-roar.

"Mistress Anne, you have a visitor," she called out to the room at large, her voice echoing off the walls.

Anne turned to see a three year old boy standing quite near Harley. As she approached, however, the child's smile turned to a look of determination as he searched the rubble and found a long, pointed stake of wood.

"What the hell?" she shouted as she surged forward in alarm. She lifted the compelling charm she'd put on Harley to make him sleep, and he awoke with a start, staring at the urchin who wished his death.

"I told you already, you little brat, I don't want to become a mere human again," he said as he grabbed the other end of the stake with little effort. "I am happy with Anne."

"Go, then, abomination," he squeaked with high-pitched disgust. "Go from this city with your ill-gotten knowledge, and plague us no more with your presence. Better to die here and now and be human than to live among the dwellers of hell."

"You of all people know hell is a myth," Harley scoffed. "I thank you for all you've taught me in the past. If you ever decide to leave here and face the real world again, look me up. Maybe there are a few things I could teach you as well."

With a dubious smirk, the youngster turned and ran quickly away, looking back as he reached the door. "Good luck, Oleuth," he said. "May you heal the world enough to make an old man like me want to find you again."

"Good-bye, Master," he said. "And thank you."

)0(

"My father is sure to give us the warriors we need," Lodan said as they stood outside the entrance to his city. "We will come above to protect you from the minions, but I swear we will leave the task of ending the life of the feral to you, Harley."

"I appreciate all that you've done so far, Lodan, but I do not wish to see you killed," Harley insisted. "Are you certain that you wish to do this?"

"I've always wished to see the outer world anyway," he said with a smile. "Besides, it was my vow as well as my mate's to make certain you succeed."

The four of them passed inside the city and a cry went up announcing their return. Several of the soldiers came out to escort them in to the king. Lodan's companions bowed as he himself grasped his father's claws in his own.

"It is good to see you, sire," he said. "But this journey has not yet reached its end."

"Rest, my son," he answered. "Stay awhile. The next leg of your journey can wait until you've had a good meal and regaled us with what has passed thus far."

"As you wish," he agreed, and turned to face Oledana with a smile. "We'll be sleeping in our own furs tonight, *lialit*. Toluth, show my companions to a better lodging than they had before. I want them given fresh blood to drink, and a full repast as well. And then, do not disturb them tonight. I'm sure they are quite— hungry."

Anne and Harley cast each other a salacious grin, and the pair of them both winked at Lodan over these words. He raised a claw at them, and then took Oledana into his arms and flew away, the smile on his face almost as brilliant as the fire in the main hearth.

)0(

"I hate taking this break," Harley said uneasily as he and Anne sat comfortably on a large bed of furs. They'd been in the posh room all of fifteen minutes, and she'd only just managed to get him to sit down.

"What harm is there in it?" she wanted to know. "It will take us more time to get to the surface, and then we have to discover where the feral is. I don't think he will have left Los Angeles. He's hoping that you'll show your face again, so he will have waited for you there. But, the real question is, will we find him, or will he find us first?"

"If I'm right about this, we need to find Strumpkull," said Harley as he looked at her. "He turned him, and has compelled him to kill me. It's Strumpkull who will be looking—and he is who I intend to find. When his maker is dead, will Strumpkull's compelling end?"

"It's difficult to say," Anne said. "It depends on how strongly he has been compelled, and how strongly he wishes to break free of it."

"He was so excited to have been turned, he may not wish to break the compelling at all."

"That is a problem," she agreed. "But it is a problem we can save for the surface, my love. For now, I want you inside me. I want to make love to you for hours, to know that we're nearing the end of this whole mess, and we'll soon be able to do whatever we wish."

"I've still got to come back to do a service for the king, you know," he reminded her.

"I have not forgotten about him," she said. "But the king is not in my bed, and you are. Who do you think I'd rather spend my concentration on right now?"

Looking at the hunger on her face, Harley could not help but chuckle. "I think I might have a pretty good idea," he answered. "It might be kind of fun watching you fuck the king."

"Beast!" she shouted in surprise as she swatted his tickling fingers away, moving quickly out of the bed. "You want me in another man's bed?"

"Of course not," he teased her, capturing her in his arms. "He's not a man, he's a demon."

Laughing with him, she said, "Mm, yes, a huge, smelly, bald, wrinkly demon. And his wingtips really turn me on. He's just so damned hot."

Harley laughed. "You want that huge demonic cock all the way in, so it comes out the top end. That's be so good."

Anne grimaced. "That is too much," she told him. "I think I much prefer a more manageable appendage."

"You mean like this one?" he asked as he rubbed it against her belly.

"The very one," she answered as she took it out and fondled it. "The only one."

"Your wish is my command," he chuckled, and carried her back to bed.

Chapter Forty-Two

Oledana and Lodan were lying on their furs. She was comfortably ensconced in the crook of his arm, with a soft smile playing about her well-sated lips. He contemplated her for a while, and then she looked up at him curiously.

"What is it, Lodan?" she wanted to know.

"I was thinking about something that Anne said to me," he confessed, smirking as the corners of her smile turned quickly down.

"And what might that be?" she inquired with sweet venom.

"*Lialit*, please, you flatter me," he said. "She is a vampire. I would not want her the way I want you."

"What did she say?" Oledana asked in exasperation.

"She told me that she and Harley have an undying fire," he said, looking into her eyes. "And then she said that perhaps we did, too. I don't know, we demons are so practical. Do you think it is truly possible for us to love?"

"It must be," she answered softly.

"Why?" he asked, chucking her under her chin.

"Because I love you, Lodan," she admitted. "I would never want another mate in my bed. So promise me that you won't get yourself killed."

Lodan smirked again. "I love you, too, little one. And I will not get myself killed. You can be sure of that."

Content beyond measure, Oledana nestled into his arms again, and they drifted off to sleep.

)0(

"Right there!" Anne shouted happily. Harley pressed into her flesh just a bit more, easing the tension in her sore shoulders for her. "Mm, Harley, nobody does that better than you. They can't possibly, because you are the best."

"I can think of something else to press," he mentioned with a smile.

"You've pressed that for three hours already," she told him tiredly. "I thought we were supposed to get some rest while we were here."

"And I thought that you told me to do something to keep my mind off what we'll be doing up top," he pointed out. "It's a fair trade-off, considering the amount of pleasuring you're getting as a result."

"Yes, I suppose it is," she agreed. "But even vampires could use a little sleep."

"Just one last time?" he coaxed her.

"Mm, don't call it that," she said in distaste. "Call it one more time before sleeping instead."

Harley moved over top of her and lay gently on the top, kissing her soundly. Anne wrapped both her arms and legs around him, pulling him as close as she could and reveling in his touch. She could never seem to get enough of touching him.

"You are the most beautiful woman who ever lived," Harley whispered against her hair. "I don't know how I would ever exist without you."

"Nor I, you," she whispered back. "I just know this time the battle will be different. This time, we're going to be more prepared."

"Shh!" he whispered and slid his tongue into her mouth, tasting all the crevices he found there. "I'm going to take you one more time—and maybe one more after that as well."

Anne giggled at this, and then moaned his name as he slid inside her wet hole. She may have been claiming she wanted to sleep, but her anatomy was telling him a different story all its own.

"I could never get enough of you, my sweet, sweet Vivianne," he said with all his heart. "Not even in my dreams."

He made love to her then. She went wild with need as he slid into her, moving with him for all she was worth. He flipped them over so that she was on top, and proceeded to pound into her, making her come with a quick, excited gasp as she held on to him.

"So good!" she breathed when he kissed her before he pulled out. Then, realizing the kiss had gotten him going yet again, to slide right back in, ready for more.

Anne sobbed with pleasure right into his mouth. He reached out and caressed her thigh, coaxing her to put it back around him. She was so hot and so wet she complied without the least bit of hesitation.

"Yes, yes Harley! Make me come again!" Anne practically screamed as she fell against him.

And he did exactly that.

Chapter Forty-Three

The streets of L.A. seemed fairly quiet at the two vampires stepped out of the cave and out into the middle of the grassy park. Anne smiled as she realized that the silly humans had no idea they were walking past a gateway to a whole other word.

Holding back just inside the exit, the twelve demons waited for the signal to advance. They had all agreed that they should go straight to Demetrius's castle in search of him. He was almost certain to know the whereabouts of the man they sought.

"Okay, the coast is clear," Harley said. "Now, how did you intend to get twelve demons across the green and find a vehicle to stash them in?"

Lodan raised a brow as he smirked at the lesser child smugly. "We'll fly, of course," he said as he motioned to the others. "No human would be crazy enough to inform the authorities if they saw a large group of demons fly past. They'd be declared insane."

"You've been up here before," Harley said appreciatively. "Lead on, my friend."

Everyone flew straight up into the air and swiftly crossed the field. They landed in the parking lot, and before Harley was even on his feet, Lodan had discovered a van with the keys hidden in the visor.

"That is fucking incredible," Harley had to tell him. "But maybe we should steal two vehicles instead of one. I don't think we all fit—never mind."

As he'd spoken, each of the spare demons and transformed from huge creatures to creatures the size of imps. "How did they do that? I didn't know demons were shapeshifters."

"Not all of them are," Lodan told him. "This troop is hand-picked. Only the best were chosen for this task. After all, they must protect the future heir."

"Like you need to be protected," Harley scoffed.

"I do not speak of myself," he said in a proud voice. "I am referring to my future child."

Oledana blushed when she heard his words, and said, "Stop it, Lodan. They didn't need to know about that right now. We've got bigger things to do."

"Can I not be proud, *lialit?*"

"Of course you can," she answered happily. "I want you to be proud."

"Harley, you know the way. You drive," said Lodan as he got inside and sat in the back with the others.

"Yeah, that's not a bad idea," he commented. "We'd be awfully suspicious looking with a huge red guy at the wheel either way. Oh hey, you shrank down too."

Harley gunned the engine, and soon they were on the road. He drove right up to the castle gates and pressed through, pulling to a stop several feet away from the building. Each being exited the vehicle and regrew, and then Lodan and Harley both turned to their women.

"Stay here in the car," Lodan told Oledana. "Anne, you will keep her safe. I do not want to find out she's been in this brawl. If she would have allowed me to leave her home, she would not even be here."

"This was my quest in the first place," the young demoness insisted. "It would be ridiculous to expect you to finish it for me."

"I have made this quest my own, just as you have," he told her. "Now just stay in the car and stop trying to argue. I don't want to have to be worried about you during this battle."

"We don't even know if there's about to be a battle," she pointed out.

"No, my dear, I can smell a good battle a mile away," he said. "Do you not smell all those vampires near here?"

"I will keep her safe," said Anne, even though she felt a strong urge to point out that there were supposed to be many vampires here, and he might very well be smelling them. "Just go guard Harley and don't give us another thought."

Lodan leaned in and kissed Oledana, then grasped Anne's hand and gave it a squeeze. She nodded at him, and then he was gone.

"What was that all about?" Oledana wanted to know.

"You and I have other plans, my dear," Anne explained. "We need to cast a binding spell."

"You have everything we need?" she inquired.

"Everything but the feral," Anne said with a glint of steel in her eye. "Him, we're going to have to acquire last."

The two females bent over a caldron with their heads together, completely hidden from anyone outside the van. And, as it turned out, that was a good thing because as they worked about fifty vampires passed by and disappeared into the brush. The same brush in which the demons were already lying in wait.

"Did you hear that?" whispered Oledana as she peeked out one of the windows. "I think someone's out there."

"A whole lot of someones," agreed Anne. "Keep down, and keep quiet. Let's just get this potion done. I have a feeling Harley is going to need it soon."

Anne poured the liquid into three different vials, and hid two of them under the front seats of the van, one on each side. The third she kept with her, slipping it neatly between her breasts just as someone opened the door.

"Well, well, look who we have here," said Strumpkull as he opened the sliding door. "A really hot chick, and her pet dog."

"Don't insult Anne like that," said Oledana as she puffed up to her most intimidating, which for her just wasn't quite enough to strike the fear into her enemy's heart that she was hoping for.

"Don't, Oledana," said Anne as she shrewdly watched the fledgling and his men. "We cannot hope to win this battle—

at least, we cannot win it here."

"Search the van," Strumpkull instructed the five vampires he had with him. In the background, the sounds of a pitched battle met their ears. "I've got a feeling that where this little lady is, Harley will follow. Maybe—" and here he grabbed Anne by the arm, "—he'll come where we take her now."

"You're damn right he will," she told him as they walked. "And he's going to bring an ass-kicking with him."

"We'll see about that," Strumpkull scoffed. "But I always was pretty good in my martial arts class."

"You forgot to bring my demon," Anne pointed out.

"We want Trent to follow you, not his hoard of demons," he explained. "The demon girl stays here. Maybe we can stop the army before it even gets started. Lord Tybeth, you deal with the little demon problem. I've got bigger fish to fry."

As they got into a different car and Strumpkull started the engine, Anne could hear the sounds of battle coming to a stop. Lodan would not want his mate harmed, she was sure. The help they'd brought along was surely now at an end.

Chapter Forty-Four

Harley stepped inside the old warehouse by the docks, more cautious than ever. Even though he knew it did him no good against the feral in particular, he had his gun drawn. He checked each point as he walked, ready to fire on anything that came out him, at least to slow whatever it was down.

In the background, a faucet was dripping. The steady plopping sound began to get on his nerves. Unexpectedly, Lazzo stepped out of the shadows.

"Hello, Harley," he said with a smile. "We knew you would come."

"What, you mean you're on the feral's side?" said the surprised fledgling. "I never would have thought that you'd let anyone have control over you."

"Trust me, Harley, I am not under anyone's control," he answered with a laugh. "It's such a shame your memories have not yet returned. It leaves us so many topics of which we cannot talk."

"Oh no, Lazzo," said Harley as the other man fell into step beside him. "Why don't you enlighten me?"

"Enlighten you?" he repeated, laughing again. "Oh, all right. Why not?" Moving stealthily with him, Lazzo said, "You were not originally made by Anne, Harley. There was another man in her life then, and it was that man who chose you. You were smart—cunning, even. You were a mage with so much knowledge, you would have been very useful to him. If only he could control you. Possess you."

Harley glanced at him, hard. "No one can possess me."

"Yes, that appears to be the case," he agreed. "But back then, long ago, you were much more—experimental—than you are in this incarnation. You were your maker's lover, in fact. And oh, how he did love you. He thought perhaps the two of you possessed the undying fire, but no, you had to go and choose Anne."

"The undying fire?" Harley said. "Anne is the only one I could ever love. Only she can possess my heart."

"And why should that be?" Lazzo said, more impassioned now. "Why can't a person give that fire to more than one other? Everything would have been fine if you would just have loved me, too."

Harley stopped walking, and turned to look at him. "Loved you, too? Loved you?" he said as he pulled a stake from his trench coat. "Who are you to me, Lazzo? Were you the one who made me? Were you the one who has been haunting my dreams? Was it you who has been killing everyone in sight? Are you the feral I seek?"

"Don't do this, Harley," he begged as tears stung at his eyes. "Don't battle me again. We don't have to be enemies, you and I."

"Yes, you do," Anne said as she stepped out of hiding, surprising them both.

"What happened to Strumpkull, Vivianne?" Lazzo demanded hotly as he began to back cautiously away.

"I gave him the slip."

Harley spared only a moment to think about the future Strumpkull looked forward to. He could not allow himself to be distracted by such eventualities here. "What are you doing here, Anne?"

"Oh, didn't you know, Harley?" she scoffed. "Wherever I am, you are sure to follow. They've led you here hoping for your death. But there's something that they didn't count on. They didn't know that I'd be free to give you this."

Before he even knew what was happening, Anne pulled a little vial out and kissed him as she put it in his hand. "Bind him," she whispered into his ear as she backed away."

"That was your protection, woman?" Lazzo scoffed. "You think that giving him a kiss is going to save him? How pathetic. It didn't work before, and it will not work now. Take her. If she tries to interfere again, kill her."

Strumpkull stepped out, and Anne allowed him to grab her arm without a fight. Then Lazzo moved forward, fangs coming out as he rounded on Harley.

"The scary looking fangs thing doesn't frighten me anymore, Lazzo," Harley told him. "You may have given me nightmares in the past, but right now, we're in the present."

Fog began to fill the room, making everything difficult to see. Harley waved his hand, calling forth wind with a powerful mage spell.

"What the hell did you do?" gasped Lazzo. "You've regained your magic?"

"I've regained a great deal more than that," Harley said as he surged forward. "I've discovered the key to tranquility."

With a powerful thrust, Harley jammed the vial of fluid into Lazzo's mouth. With his other hand, he brought his wooden stake up into his heart.

Blood spurted out his mouth as he stared up in surprise. "Harley, what did you do?"

"I just made you into a model citizen," Harley told him with a malevolent grin. "From now on, you're going to be the nicest reincarnated vampire the world has ever known."

"Damn you," he breathed. "Damn you to hell."

"I heard hell was a pretty nice place," Harley said. "Maybe I'll even take Vivianne there with me. We could use a vacation after chasing down your dumb ass."

The light left Lazzo's eyes. His soul flew free, floating far above the scene. For the first time in forever, he felt good. He owed Harley Trent the rest of his lives. Perhaps someday he'd repay him. Perhaps someday they'd meet again.

Epilogue

"How is she doing?" Harley asked worriedly as he and Lodan hurried to talk to the nurse who had stepped outside. The two males cast each other a worried glance.

"She's just fine, and so are your two new babies," the female pronounced with a grin.

"Two?" Lodan gasped, casting Harley a look of surprise. "That's quite impressive."

"Yes, it is," he agreed, starting to pace about again.

"You're going to wear away the cave floor doing that," Lodan said. "Why don't we just go in there and see her?"

"Yes, of course," Harley agreed.

They stepped into the structure in which the new babies had been born. Each picked up a bundle and held it up.

"Both boys," the nurse said with a smile as she left them there and returned to other duties.

"Two sons," Harley said. "That's a pretty big responsibility."

"Yes, it is," Lodan agreed as he uncovered the face of the boy in his arms. "I think this one has your eyes. Probably your hair as well."

"They have my colors, but other than that, I think these two look very much like their mother," Harley said with a smile.

"Well, you had better hope their features toughen up a bit," the demon said. "You don't want the other children to pick on them for looking too feminine."

"Lodan, they're vampire children," he pointed out. "The other children will pick on them no matter what."

"Only until they hear about how tough their father is," he pointed out.

Harley chuckled as he stepped over to see Anne, who was fast asleep in her bed. After so many hours pushing these two out, that did not surprise him overmuch.

"And if that's not enough, they could also point out that you're the future king's best friend," Lodan added with pride.

"Yes," Harley agreed. "I bet that would be all they had to say."

About the Author

Robin Joy Wirth has been in love with the written word ever since she first learned to spell the word "you" at the tender age of two. She has a very lively, active fantasy world of which this book is but a small part. Robin invites readers to join her there in everything from fantasy to history to science fiction stories, usually generously flavored with a bit of romance.

The mother of four children of varying ages, she resides in Washington state with the wonderful hero of her very own romance.

Made in the USA
Charleston, SC
01 August 2014